THE POPE

CARDS OF LOVE

LP LOVELL

PROLOGUE

'For even Satan disguises himself as an angel of light.' - 2
Corinthians 11:14

My arm swings back and smashes into his face. I smile at the
satisfying crunching of his cheekbone, and the little demon
that I try to keep leashed dances around his fire. My fist
pulls back again and again, nailing him in the gut, the ribs,
mainly body shots. And when he's lying on the floor gasping
for short breaths through cracked ribs and straining lungs, I
pause. My chest rises and falls heavily, and my knuckles are
bleeding where the brass knuckles have bitten into my skin.
I don't care. His blood and mine mix together, coating my
fist and smearing up the length of my forearm.

That demon is riding me hard, screaming at me to just
land one last punch to his throat. Collapse his trachea, and
watch him suffocate to death right before my eyes.

I walk away, pacing for a few minutes. His fingers grip
the arm of the couch, and I notice the splits in his right
knuckles. From hitting her. Glancing across the room, I spot

some kind of bronze statue on his mantelpiece, an award of sorts. Picking it up, I toss it up and down in my hand, testing the weight.

Then I grab his wrist, wrenching him forward on a cry and slamming his palm on the coffee table.

"What are you—"

My arm arcs high into the air, and I bring the statue down hard over his hand. I swear I can hear the bones crack, and I smile. He screams, and I slam a hand over his mouth.

"Shut the fuck up." Tears form and fall down his cheeks, meeting my fingers. When he finally quiets, I remove my hand, and he whimpers like a kicked dog. "Stay away from her, or I'll make this look like a trip to Disneyland," I growl.

"You're fucking her, aren't you?" His voice is pained. I say nothing, allowing the assumption to go unchecked. "Does she know who you are?" Each word is a strained whisper.

Dropping to a crouch, I grab a handful of his hair and wrench his head back. "*You* know who I am. And I know exactly who you are, who you work for, your entire tiny network. Go near her again, and I will destroy you." I stand, sneering at him. "You should be grateful I'm showing you mercy." I remove the knuckles and slip them into my pocket. "After all, I am a man of God."

1

DELILAH

I LIFT the glass of wine to my lips, chugging half of it in several large gulps. Awkward doesn't come close to describing the way I'm feeling. My father cuts a piece of steak off, shoving it in his mouth, utterly oblivious to the tension in the room.

Sabrina, also known as 'that whore'— a direct quote from my mother — sits across from me in a dress worthy of Elizabeth Taylor. She picks through a green salad, and I roll my eyes. The woman looks like Skeletor. She could do with a decent steak.

"Aren't you going to eat, Delilah?" my father asks.

"I'm not hungry," I mumble, taking another gulp of my wine.

"You shouldn't drink on an empty stomach. You'll get drunk." God. Yes. Please. This shit may just about become bearable.

I offer a polite, yet hostile smile. "Your concern is touching."

Clearing his throat, he swipes a napkin over his mouth and steeples his fingers in front of him. Sabrina jumps up like a trained dog and swipes his empty plate, scuttling away with it.

"I have to say. I'm surprised you called." His eyes meet mine, the exact shade of grey as my own. His thinning salt and pepper hair is neatly combed, his shirt immaculate, cufflinks gleaming. "I didn't think you'd accept my invitation for dinner."

Lifting the wine to my lips again, I mumble, "Whatever gave you that idea?"

He releases a sigh, and behind his glasses, scowl lines sink into the corners of his eyes. "I know that your mother —"

I hold my hand up, placing the glass down on the pristine white tablecloth. "Please spare me the speech." My mother is no prize, but even so, at the age of fifteen, I was disgusted to find out that my dad had been banging his secretary for two years. He moved to London, married that piece of trash, and I was lucky if I heard from him once a month. This is the fourth time I've seen him in as many years, and the last time we spoke was at least six months ago.

I'd rather not be here, but he is paying for my degree and expects me to attend when summoned. That's the one thing my father is good for: money. He's one of the top neurosurgeons in the country, so his time and attention is hard fought, but his guilt money? Not so much.

"I'm changing my degree," I blurt. He frowns, his lips pressing into a hard line. Butterflies flutter gleefully in my chest, and I fight a smile. I've pictured this moment so many times. Dreamed about it. Me; telling Henry Thomas that his only child will not be following in his egotistical footsteps. "To philosophy." Ah, and there it is. The shock, the horror, and finally the pure, trembling rage.

"What?" His voice is flat, but I hear the slight quiver in it. It takes everything in me not to smile.

"I really found myself in Thailand, and I don't want to be a doctor anymore." It's a lie. I didn't find myself. I simply questioned why I was trying so hard to please a man who doesn't give a shit. Truthfully, I don't know what I want out of life. I never have.

His face turns a worrying shade of red. "You've always wanted to be a doctor."

"No, you wanted me to be a doctor."

"That's enough, Delilah," he snaps. "I realise that I've made mistakes, but —"

"But nothing! You save peoples lives, and that's amazing, but you can't even show your own daughter a fraction of the attention that you give to strangers." I shake my head. "I don't want to be like you."

The red is tingeing on purple now, and his entire frame is trembling. "This isn't a joke. Your future is on the line here."

"No, it's not a joke."

There's a long beat of silence, and I can feel his rage encroaching through the room. There's a part of me that regresses right back to being a little girl, terrified of my father's wrath.

And then he says those words. "I never thought you would be such a disappointment, Delilah."

A knot lodges in my stomach, and I swallow down the uncomfortable feeling. All at once I'm ten-years-old again. Picking up the wine glass, I drain the remnants and push to my feet. The room tilts and sways a little.

"Good talk, Dad." I head towards the door.

"Delilah!" he shouts, and I still out of habit. "I will not pay for this. You will not throw your life away."

"I don't need you."

I walk out of the room, and with each step I take, the tension in my stomach eases. I've gone against the grain, defied my father, upset the status quo. I have no plan from here on out. A year ago, I was resigned to the path my life would take, but now...now there are just so many possibilities. I embrace the chaos of the unknown with open arms, bathing in the rebellion of it all.

Once outside, I shoot a text to Izzy. Ten minutes later, her electric blue Mini Cooper comes screaming around the corner of my father's cobblestone street. She slams to a halt beside me and winds down her window. A cloud of smoke exits the car, and she giggles, her copper red hair falling over her face.

"How did it go down?"

"Like I forced him to eat dog shit."

She laughs and slaps her hand over the steering wheel. "Get in. I have tequila shots with your name on them."

I get in her car, nearly choking on the scent of cigarette smoke. She cranks her radio and peels away from the expensive London street, leaving it all in the rearview mirror.

Isabelle pats my thigh. "I'm proud of you, Lila! Now you can become a stripper, meet a bad boy and elope, have his love child..."

I smile at my wild friend. Isabelle is beautiful, uninhibited, free — with a hunger for life that I've envied from the moment I met her. We happened upon each other two years ago, in Thailand of all places. She was travelling with a group of friends, and I was alone on a gap year because I'm always alone. I wanted to experience the world. They wanted to hit every full moon party they could find for a year. Izzy's changed my life really. She brings out the side of me that I try to keep buried: the rebel, the anarchist. She makes me embrace something that I've always believed to be bad, but it's not. It's good. So, so good.

We pull up outside an Irish bar that Izzy likes, though I have no idea why. The clientele are mostly shady characters. But they do have pool tables, so I suppose there's that. Izzy walks straight up to the bar, slamming her hand on it.

"Tequila shots!" she practically shouts at the barman. "Four." Her gaze lifts over my shoulder, a slow smile making its way over her lips. "Make that six."

"If you're ordering tequila..." A voice behind me starts. Glancing over my shoulder, I see Tiffany. She's glaring at Izzy, her hands on her hips. Wild blonde hair spills everywhere, and the buttoned shirt she's wearing falls open at the collar, hanging off her shoulder. "Every time, I tell her I do not do tequila. Then she tells me to man up, I do it, and I'm dying the next day."

I laugh. "You are aware that I share this pain?"

Izzy slides shots in front of us. "Come on. We're celebrating Lila's freedom."

"Oh, you told your Dad, Lila?"

"Yep." I lift the shot glass of golden liquid. "To doing a shit degree that there is no way to make a career out of."

We clink glasses and knock them back.

"I cannot believe you won't be in classes with me anymore. It sucks," Tiff says, wrinkling her nose against the vile taste.

"Tiff, we're living together this year. You'll see more of me." I met Tiff last year in a biology class. She's sweet and caring and fun. The three of us just spent the summer in Vietnam, and in a week's time, we'll all be moving in together for the academic year. The only difference being that I've moved from medical sciences to philosophy. From a mapped future to the spontaneity of the here and now, and nothing more.

A Corona is shoved in my hand courtesy of Izzy before she strolls over to one of the pool tables. She waves at a guy, and he lifts a hand to her in greeting. He's wearing a leather jacket and a smile that spells trouble.

"Isabelle," he greets when they get close. "Want to play?" Somehow I don't think he means pool. She picks up a pool cue, propping it against her hip.

"Sure. Who's your friend, Max?"

My attention turns to another guy leaning against the wall, and when it does, I find him looking at me. He's all lean muscles, tattoos and attitude. His dark hair matches the deep chocolate of his irises, which are currently focused on me like I'm prey. He looks like a Hollister model that's done jail time. Bad. Dangerous. Rebellious. And gorgeous. Izzy always jokes that I love a bad boy, and she's not wrong. This one is calling to me. Pushing off the wall, he moves closer, his every motion screaming of arrogance.

"I'm Nate," he says, his focus entirely on me, though I'm not the one who asked the question.

"Lila," I breathe. His lips quirk to one side before falling back into that troublesome smile.

"Want to play, Lila?" He hands me the pool cue, and our fingers brush as I take it from him. My pulse quickens, and my skin tingles. I do, very much.

Call it a weakness, or perhaps it's just text book daddy issues, but guys like him...I can't seem to say no to. It's almost like I enjoy the thrill, followed by the heartbreak — because they are always, always heartbreak. Boys like that can't be tamed, and only a foolish girl tries. So, what does that make me? An idiot, a glutton for punishment, or perhaps I'm just a junkie for that little rush they provide, for the moment they look at you as though you're the only girl in the world? It may be fleeting, but so is life, made up of hundreds of thousands of moments. For every good one, there's a bad one, and that's what men like Nate are: a double-edged sword that I seem willing to cut myself on.

I line up the breaking shot, bending over the table in front of him. "What are you going to give me if I win?" Glancing over my shoulder, I flash him a smile. His eyes shift from my arse to my face.

"What do you want?"

"Call it a drink?"

He cocks a brow. "If you girls win, I'll buy you a drink. If I win, I want a kiss."

Izzy lets out a sharp bark of laughter.

"What is this? High school?" Tiff pipes up from the nearby bar stool she's adopted.

I shrug. I haven't lost a game of pool since I was sixteen. He's not getting that kiss.

Fifteen minutes later and my five-year winning streak comes to a grinding halt. I'm a woman of my word, so Nate gets his kiss.

Six months later...

I move through the hot press of sweaty bodies, grinding and writhing against one another. Music pulses and throbs through the thick, cloying air, like a living thing, infecting everyone in the packed club.

My tight dress rides up my thighs with every step, and several stray sets of hands brush my waist, my hips, my bare legs. Through the crowd, I spot Tiff at one of the tables. She waves, beckoning me over.

"You came." She throws her arms around my neck, a drunken smile on her face.

"Yeah. Where's Izzy?"

"Last I saw she was with Charlie."

I roll my eyes. Izzy's new beau is Charles Stanley, the son of some high-ranking general. He's the good guy, the star rugby player, the smart kid. He's not her usual type, but then Izzy isn't picky. She falls in love, then gets bored and does it all over again. She says the soul doesn't have a type, nor does it commit beyond a single moment, it simply feels. It seems that it currently *feels* Charles Stanley. Then again, beneath that golden exterior, there's a streak of rebellion, a party animal. And Izzy does love a party.

Glancing around the room, I spot Nate standing at the bar; his elbows braced behind him and a bottle of beer hanging from one hand. That dangerous aura of his is like a magnet to me, and everyone around him. Our eyes meet, his lips pulling up in the small, sexy smile that made me fall so hard for him in the first place. Turning his head, he speaks to someone beside him, his gaze remaining fixed on me. Money exchanges hands, and when I track the movement that I realise it's Charles.

"There you are!" My attention snaps from the guys to Isabelle. She's wearing a white dress that barely makes it past her arse. Her gaze shifts over my shoulder to where I was looking. "That boy is all the best kinds of wrong, Lila." I roll my eyes. She grins and then pets my crotch like it's a damn cat. "I'm so happy for you."

"I swear to God, Izzy, if you are talking to my vagina..."

She laughs. "Well, I'm happy for you too."

"Yeah, well, you remember that when I'm sobbing into ice cream."

She shrugs one shoulder. "Got to take the rough with the smooth. It's the circle of life."

"Did you just quote Lion King at me?"

"Hey, the entire point of Disney is to promote great life mantras. I'm not ashamed."

"Your hippy shit is getting out of control."

She shoves a drink in my hand. "You're just trying to dull my sparkle." She sniffs. "Now drink up, buttercup."

I eye the pink liquid. "Did you spike it?" Wouldn't be the first time. Just last month she made brownies, and I foolishly thought she'd randomly taken up baking.

"You're no fun, Lila. Not since you found the street life." She laughs, her eyebrows bouncing up and down conspiratorially. She tips her own drink back and then grabs my hand, tugging me towards the dance floor, along with Tiffany. They dance together, and I watch them, but my focus is elsewhere. Glancing over my shoulder, I see Charles and Nate slap hands before Charles starts walking towards us. Nate meets my gaze and nods.

I turn my attention to Charles, and he offers me a smile, flashing perfect teeth to match his baby blues. His hand drags through golden hair, flashing the expensive watch on his wrist. He's the archetypical privileged guy in every way that matters.

As I head towards him, my stomach knots and a little shot of adrenaline enters my bloodstream. I think it's the danger, the possibility of being caught, knowing I'm doing something wrong. With every step, my heartbeat picks up. Sliding my hand into the top of my bra, I pinch a tiny plastic bag between two fingers and ball it in my fist. Charles stops in front of me, a wide smile on his face as he pulls me into an embrace. He smells clean like cologne and top-shelf vodka.

My arms wrap around his waist, and I slide the tiny plastic bag into the back pocket of his jeans. To anyone watching us, we look like friends or maybe lovers embracing, when in reality, I barely know him, and certainly not well enough to be hugging him. I paint a smile on my face, keeping up the farce as I pull away and shift past him. We go our separate ways, and I walk over to where Nate lingers at the bar.

Dark eyes track me the entire way, roaming over my body as though he owns every inch of it. His t-shirt pulls tight over his muscled physique, the pristine white material contrasting with the black ink that covers his entire right arm. From the moment I saw him in that dirty bar, all dark hair, tanned skin, tattoos, and cocky attitude, I was like a fish on a hook. Sliding his palm to my back, he wrenches me up against him, forcing me to straddle one thigh.

"I want to break his arms for touching you," he murmurs in my ear before his teeth scrape my neck. My body flushes, and a trembling breath leaves my lips.

"That wouldn't be very good for your business, would it?"

He grabs my jaw, pushing me back just a few inches before slamming his lips over mine. His tongue invades my mouth, claiming, demanding, taking what he wants. "You look fucking hot in that dress, Lila." His free hand slides up the length of my thigh, pushing under my skirt. He nips my bottom lip and then steps back, picking his beer up again.

I steady myself on the edge of the bar before my legs threaten to give out. Nate orders me a drink and slides it in front of me with a wink. Picking up the raspberry Martini, I take a sip and relish in the sweetness mixing with the bite of alcohol.

"They're in for a wild night," he says, his eyes trained off to the side of the room. I follow his gaze to Charles, who is now sitting at a table with Isabella. She places something in her mouth and washes it down with a shot of what looks like tequila. I frown, something uncomfortable pulling at my gut.

Nate places a finger beneath my chin, forcing me to look at him. "You did great, baby." He kisses my jaw. "You're good at this."

I can't pinpoint when I decided that working with Nate was a good idea. It was a few months before I realised that the all-nighters, the nice car, the lack of a 9-5 job, all equated to the fact that he's a drug dealer. Logically, I should have walked away, but that defiant streak in me only wanted him more. The badder the better, right? Then the opportunity arose to do a little side work and I figured, why not? My father had cut me off, and it is exceptionally easy money. But honestly, it really has nothing to do with the cash. It's the rush, the thrill of doing something illegal. That feeling of adrenaline pumping through your veins because this might be the time you get caught. I've always been the good girl. Sweet little Delilah who is going to be a doctor. Whose daddy is a brain surgeon. From a perfect family. Only now, I'm none of those things, and I love it. If I get caught... it would suck, but I can't help but smile as I picture my father's face. The horror. The disappointment.

There's a twisted satisfaction in it all, a sense of abandonment that I relish in — because I simply don't care. And that...is freedom.

2

DELILAH

Bright morning light streams through the windows, and I blink, rolling away from it. Sliding my hand across the sheets, I find they're still warm, and the scent of Nate's cologne lingers on them.

When I get downstairs, I find him sitting at the breakfast bar in only a pair of jeans, a cup of coffee in hand. He's splitting his attention between the television on the counter, which is tuned into some weekend breakfast show, and Summer, Izzy's cousin and our fourth housemate. She's hovering around him like a fly, twirling a strand of fake blonde hair around her finger.

"Oh, hi, Lila." Summer and I, do not like each other.

Nate holds his hand out to her, and she plucks a small bag of pills from his palm.

"Thanks, Nate." She smiles wide and leaves the kitchen, her hips swaying beneath the tiny sundress she's wearing. He turns his attention back to the TV without blinking.

"Thanks, Nate," I mimic, rolling my eyes.

Shaking my head, I go to the coffee machine. Nate loops

an arm around my waist as I move past him and presses a kiss into the side of my neck.

"Are you jealous?" he asks, amusement lacing his voice.

I cock a brow. "I don't do jealous, Nate." But I do imagine what Summer's face would look like with a broken nose.

"You sure? Because it's kind of hot."

"You're a psycho." I smirk.

He wrenches me forward, bringing his lips to my ear. "So are you, baby. You just hide it better."

I push away from him. "Stop trying to distract me. You can't just hand your shit out to anyone who asks." His hands work under my top, and his lips cruise along my collarbone as he ignores me. "That's how you get arrested. I've seen these undercover police shows."

He snorts and grabs the front of his t-shirt that I'm wearing, tugging me close. My hands land on his chest and the rich scent of coffee wafts around me. "You worry too much."

His lips hit my neck, and my eyes drift to the TV. I still, and it's as though the very blood in my veins has turned to ice. My chest knots so hard, I can't catch a full breath, and my heart lets out stuttered, heavy thuds.

"Oh my god," I whisper.

"What?"

I push away from Nate and grasp the edge of the counter, fighting back the bile that's creeping up my throat. It's no good. Whirling around, I throw up in the sink. My pounding pulse races in my ears, but I can still hear the reporter talking.

"The man and woman were found in the nightclub, Fire, in the early hours of this morning. Both were rushed to St. George's hospital but were pronounced dead on arrival. This is a suspected drug overdose, but a coroner's report will confirm. They have

been identified as Isabelle Wright, and Charles Stanley, son of General Edward Stanley."

A hand lands on my back, and I'm vaguely aware of Nate's voice, but it's a distant hum over the incessant ringing in my ears.

"It's okay." Those are the only words I can make out. It's not though. Reality crashes into me like a freight train ploughing into my chest. Isabelle is dead. Isabelle overdosed. Charles overdosed. On drugs I gave them.

"Shit," I choke. "This isn't happening."

"Lila."

"Just...I need you to go, Nate."

Staggering away from the kitchen, I go to the bathroom and lock the door. I slide to the floor and clutch my knees to my chest as the tears fall. Horror sets in like the hand of death itself wrapping around my throat. I feel sick. She's dead. I'm a killer. And nothing will ever be the same again.

***

The sunshine illuminates my fogged breath as it hits the air, and the frozen grass crunches beneath my boots. The frosted headstones sparkle like gems in the icy landscape of the cemetery. It's too bright. Too pretty.

The people gathered around the freshly dug grave seem like demons, leeching all the happiness from the world with their black clothing.

I stare numbly at the deep dark hole in the ground — her pristine white coffin sitting at the bottom. It's been two weeks since she died, and I'm not sure it's fully sunk in until now. Two weeks of this numb zombie state. Two weeks of nightmares. Two weeks of waiting for the police to knock on my door and drag me away like the killer I am.

People step forward one at a time, paying their respects and dropping roses on the coffin.

A jagged, painful lump in my throat accompanies the tears that track down my cheeks. It's become familiar to me now though. Like my guilt and grief are two strands of barbed wire that have knotted together tightly, lodging there.

I watch Isabelle's mother cling to her older brother, her sobs a sombre note ringing out through the graveyard. I watch him try to stay strong, try to hold his mother up in her hour of need, and my heart breaks for him. For them. I did that. My actions that I thought had no consequences; well, I'm looking at the consequences. A family torn apart. Two families, in fact. And Isabelle, so young and wild. She deserved better.

"Lila." I glance up at the sound of the small voice. Tiffany stands a few feet away, her hands knotted in front of her, the black skirt of her dress blowing in the wind. "Do you want a lift to the wake?"

I look back down at the coffin. "I'm not going." I've paid my respects and said goodbye, apologised to her a thousand times in my mind and hope that somehow the thoughts find their way out into the universe. Sorry isn't enough, but it's all I have, because what is a life worth? It's immeasurable.

"Are you sure?"

"I have something I have to do."

Her blonde eyebrows pinch together. "Look, Lila. We've all been hit hard by her death, but...but I know Izzy would want me to try and take care of you." She moves closer, placing a hand on my arm. "Please don't hide from me."

I nod. "Thanks." The word is flat even to my ears, but I really don't care. Turning away, I start walking. "Goodbye, Izzy," I whisper.

Wrapping my arms tightly around my body, I hunch against the biting cold that seems to have penetrated my very bones. Saturday morning shoppers and people going about their lives, pack the London streets. I've always been an outsider, a lone wolf as such, but never have I felt more removed than now. Until Izzy and Tiff, I'd never really know what it was to have true friends — to be a part of something. Izzy was good to me, kind when she didn't have to be. And now she's gone because of me. The guilt and the grief have eaten me alive for the last two weeks. But I can't handle the waiting, the not knowing.

Crossing the road, I pass through the tall metal gates that lead up to the front of Thames Police Station. A couple of police cars cruise past me before pulling up outside. I glance up at the drab-looking five-storey building with its grey concrete walls and dirty windows. Taking a deep breath, I step off the kerb but am wrenched backwards before my foot meets the tarmac road. Turning around, I come face to face with Nate, his expression twisted in a snarl.

"What the fuck are you doing?" he hisses.

His fingers wrap around my wrist in a bruising grip. I'm so numb that I don't fight him as he drags me down the road.

"Let me go."

I'm shoved into an alleyway between a bar and a restaurant and slammed up against the wall. Hot breaths rush over my face and his arm trembles as he presses it against my chest, pinning me in place.

"Fuck." He shoves away violently and paces back and forth in front of me. "What the hell are you thinking, Lila?"

"I killed her," I whisper.

He laughs, the sound, cold and cruel. "She killed herself, you stupid bitch."

"No." I shake my head.

"She took one pill too many, Lila. It happens. Your perspective is just warped."

"She's dead, Nate!" How can he possibly be blasé about this?

"Life goes on."

"I have to turn myself in." He might be able to live like this, but I can't. The guilt is like a disease, eating away at me day after day. And the anxiety; the constant looking over my shoulder, wondering when the police will knock on my door…it's killing me. I'm a mess.

He rushes me, his hand slipping around my throat and squeezing hard enough to provide an adequate warning. "You don't understand. You do that, and you risk all of us."

"I'm only turning myself in. I won't say anything about you."

A sick smile twists his lips. "Until they press you, asking who gave you the pills or who you work for. They don't want some university student with the conscience of fucking Mother Theresa. They want the dealers."

"I won't sell you out," I say flatly. Maybe I should though because it's wrong. This is all so wrong.

His eyes lock with mine, and his jaw tenses. He seems so cold now, so ruthless.

"I almost believe you." His eyes drop to my lips, and though his grip doesn't soften, he strokes a thumb over the side of my throat. "But not enough to risk it." He steps away from me, and we stand a couple of feet apart, feeling like strangers. "If you go to the police, I can't protect you from the people I work for, Lila. They won't care about what you do or don't say. You going there is enough. They'll go to any lengths to protect their business. You, me...we're all disposable."

And then he simply turns and walks away, leaving me in the dirty alleyway alone. I was prepared to turn myself in, ready to lose years of my life if it would go some way towards righting this wrong, but I don't want to die. Call it basic survival instinct. But this is all I have, my coping mechanism. I've been on auto-pilot, one foot in front of the other to get to the funeral and then here. Beyond that, I had no plan, no way to deal with this.

And where does that leave me? I can't turn myself in, but I can't live like this either. Stepping out of the alleyway, I glance to the left and spot the sign for a bar. Without much thought, I go inside and order a shot of vodka. I just need to drown everything out.

3

JUDAS

"Forgive me, Father, for I have sinned." The deep, gravelly voice rumbles from the other side of the divider. "My sins are...*grievous*." One word, completely inconspicuous to anyone who may be listening, but one particular word that tells me this man is here for business, not spiritual healing.

"I see. How many Hail Mary's do you think will absolve you?"

"Three should do it."

"Third pew from the back on the left. Usual time," I whisper, before speaking louder for anyone who might be listening. "God the Father of mercies, through the death and resurrection of His Son, has reconciled the world to Himself and sent the Holy Spirit among us for the forgiveness of sins. Through the ministry of the Church, may God give you pardon and peace. I absolve you from your sins, in the name of the Father, and of the Son and of the Holy Spirit."

"Amen," he responds, before leaving the booth.

Pulling the curtain back a fraction, I watch as he moves towards the rear of the church and slides into the pew, third from the back on the left. Dropping the curtain, I straighten as a new sinner takes a seat for confession.

"Forgive me, father, for I have sinned. It has been twelve days since my last confession," the man says.

"I will hear your confession."

There's a pause, and I smile. The petty sins are the ones they spill easily, seeking to be appeased and assured of their place behind the pearly gates. But that pause? That's the sign of a true sinner.

"I was unfaithful to my wife," he whispers. Ah, and there it is, the waft of guilt, the simperings of a tainted soul.

"And do you repent?"

"Yes, yes. I'm...truly sorry." No, he's not. He'll do the same thing, again and again, because some of us can't help ourselves. We're fundamentally flawed, drawn to the darkness. Bad people. But it's often said that God loves the sinner. He just hates the Sin.

I recite the words I've spoken a thousand times, granting him false forgiveness.

As darkness encroaches the church, I move through the aisle, placing bibles along the worn wooden lip on the back of each pew. When I reach the third pew from the back, I pick up the first prayer cushion and unzip it, removing a wad of cash inside.

Taking my phone from my pocket, I dial the first number on there.

"Yeah?"

"Bring three kilos. Third from the back. Left side." And then I hang up, picking up three of the prayer cushions and moving them. Within the next hour, one of my guys will place three kilos of cocaine in this very pew, the block the exact size as a prayer cushion and concealed within the awful crocheted fabric. An hour after that, the client who placed and paid for his order this morning, will come in and collect.

Simple. Effective. Lucrative. And all protected by the holy premise of religion.

I check my watch, and when I look up, my father is striding down the centre aisle looking like every dodgy gangster from every movie I've ever seen. His dark grey hair is combed back, his three-piece suit in place, and his shoes so shiny I could probably see my reflection in them. He pauses in front of me, saying nothing as he places a cigarette to his lips and inhales deeply.

"You can't smoke in here, old man."

His hardened face breaks into a smile and perfect white veneers stand out against tanned skin. Long ingrained lines sink into the corners of his eyes from years of laughter. "Forgive me, father, for I have sinned." He crosses himself, a hacking laugh bubbling from his throat.

"Come on." I roll my eyes, heading towards the door at the back of the church.

He follows me into the office and circles behind the desk, kicking his shiny brogues up on it. Changing out of my robes, I hang them on the back of the door. "You know," he glances around the room, swiping the rosary off the desk and dangling it from one finger, "I once saw a porno that started out like this."

I groan. Twenty-eight years of this... William Kingsley is an old-school cockney gangster. He believes in expensive suits and even more expensive booze, and in acting only to benefit himself, his business, or his family. He also takes virtually nothing seriously, but the moment he does is the moment everyone in the room sits up and pays attention.

"Can you focus?"

He only grins and rocks back and forth in the chair like an errant, bored child.

A few seconds later there's a quiet knock on the door. I open it to a scowling Harold Dawson. The older man's balding head matches the beet red of his face, and the overhead lighting reflects off it like a buffed bowling ball. He's an average upstanding member of the community: a businessman, good Catholic, charity founder, husband, and father. He and his wife attend mass every Sunday, raise funds for the local school; even foster stray dogs. He's unsuspecting. Good in every way that matters to anyone on the outside looking in. He's the perfect Trojan horse, and more than that, he's already proven.

"You're blackmailing me?" He waves a manila envelope around.

"Blackmail is such an ugly word," I say, fighting a smirk. He storms into the room, and I close the door behind him. "Harold Dawson, this is William Kingsley." I offer no further explanation than that. My father's eyes meet mine, an amused smile playing over his lips. I go by my mother's maiden name of Kavanagh, simply because the Kingsley name carries a certain reputation. My father, in particular, is infamous, with a criminal career that has spanned decades, unproven and unchecked. A priest with the name Kingsley — well that would draw too much attention and defeat my entire façade. Harold however, already has dealings with one Kingsley. Whether or not he actually knows that, I can't be sure.

Harold shifts from one foot to the other, and I can see his mind spinning, the wheels turning as he tries to piece it all together.

"I know who you are," he mumbles in Dad's direction. "What do you want with me?" He glances at me, accusation red hot in his eyes as he waves the envelope around. "Aside from fucking me in the arse."

"I want to make you money, Mr Dawson," my father says.

"I don't need more money, and I don't want yours."

"Nobody *needs* more money, Harold." He glares at me. "It's obvious, you launder money through your children's charity." I nod towards the envelope in his hand containing a simple spreadsheet of figures pulled from his very own computer. "Tsk, tsk, I didn't take you for such a sinner."

He sneers at me. "Says the priest who's trying to black-mail me."

"There's no trying. This is simple, you either sell us a twenty percent share in Global Aid, and clean our money, or I turn those figures over to the police."

His eyes go wide, but my expression remains stone cold. "You wouldn't. If you knew who I worked for..."

"Oh, I know exactly who you work for."

"Then you know that if I sell part of my company, the company they use, then this is a signed and sealed death warrant for all of us." There's genuine fear in his eyes, and I can see the erratic throbbing of his pulse at his throat. I shouldn't revel in it, but of course, I do. He shakes his head. "Turn me in. They'll kill me anyway. And you."

I crack my neck to the side, and my father's eyes meet mine. He gives the smallest shake of his head, trying to leash the temper I'm sure he can see brewing in my eyes. You see, I'm not a patient man, and I'm not accustomed to asking for things twice. Snatching the rosary off the desk, I grab Harold's shoulder and shove him into the chair.

"What—"

Moving behind him, I snap the rosary tight across his throat, clasping the beads in one fist. He flails and panics, and my father lets out an exasperated sigh.

"You should have just gone this way in the first place. Would have saved you some trouble." He smirks, but I'm not in the mood.

"Harold." I pat his shoulder, but he's too busy thrashing around, clawing at his throat. "I tried to be nice, but what you failed to see is that this wasn't a request." I release the beads, and he drags a gasping breath into his lungs.

My father pushes to his feet. "You get above market value for your twenty percent. You make more money as a cut, we get our money cleaned, and your current clients continue to get theirs cleaned. No harm, no foul."

Harold glances up, his face still puce and his breaths rattling. "You have no idea," he mutters. I drag him to his feet and shove him towards the door. He pauses for a moment, shaking his head once more before opening the door and disappearing.

I glance at my father and raise a brow. "You know he's banking on us having a bullet in our heads before the day is even out."

My father groans, taking a cigarette from his pocket. "Well, we might do, but this is your plan."

"We don't have a lot of choices. There's no sign of Fire opening any time soon, and we've already lost half our client base to those Italian fucks." I need operations back in place. I can't sell cocaine without distributors, or somewhere to clean the money. With my biggest nightclub down, the dirty money is building, and it makes me edgy.

"The police are involved." He shrugs. "The distro's are like rats fleeing a ship with a hole. You plug the hole, and they'll drown at sea."

"That doesn't help us right now."

"You could always speak to Saint. Speed things along. It won't get your clients back, but it'll fix your hole."

I laugh. "I'm not asking Saint for shit." My brother has most of London's police force in his back pocket, mainly because he pays them more than we do. I'd sooner slit my own throat before asking him for a favour though. "This will work." I'm absolutely playing with fire because Saint is the very person I'm fucking over. I sigh and drag my hand over my face. "I can handle him." But we both know it's a lie because my brother can't be *handled*. By anyone.

———

My phone rings, the shrill sound dragging me from a deep sleep.

Squinting at the screen, I see my brother's name flashing. "Yeah?"

"We need to meet." His voice is clipped as always.

"Look, it's not —"

"In person," he hisses. "Be at Confess in one hour. And Judas, don't make me find you." Then he hangs up. The clock reads one thirty in the morning. Of course, Saint doesn't exactly operate in normal business hours.

That was quick, even for him. Getting out of bed, I throw on jeans and a shirt, rolling the sleeves up past my forearms. When I leave the house the street outside is silent, the orange glow of the streetlights subtly reflecting off the wet pavements and roads. I'd rather go back to bed than make the half-hour trek to the other side of London, then again, there are a lot of things I'd prefer to do than have to meet my brother.

I reach the nightclub that my brother owns: Confess. It's a church, and the irony is not lost on me because Saint is as devout in his faith as anyone I know. Maybe that's why he bought it? He feels at home here, spiritually peaceful.

Though, I never thought I would see the day when he would welcome fornication and debauchery into a house of God. Our views differ vastly.

I park up and cross the small gravel car park to the front door. Music pulses through the air, the tones muted to a low throaty rumble. One knock on the heavy wooden door and it swings open, allowing the throbbing bass to pour out into the night air. The bouncer looks me over and nods before letting me in. The place is packed wall to wall with bodies. It's on the outskirts of the city in an undesirable area, and yet everyone wants into this club because it's exclusive and rumoured to be a hub for wealthy and corrupt individuals. Funny how the human disposition draws them to the dangerous. Like junkies seeking out a fix.

I move through the dancing bodies until I reach the back of the church and slip through the door into a hallway. At the end is a single door with a security detail. I've seen one of the guys here before, but even if they'd never laid eyes on me, they'd know I was related to Saint. We look almost exactly alike. Same blue eyes, same near-black hair, same smile. I only lack the fundamental wrongness that clings to Saint like a second skin.

Without a word, the first guy scans a card over the door. It beeps, and he steps back, allowing me to open it onto a set of stairs — the descent into hell.

The temperature drops by a few degrees when I reach the bottom, and I glance around at the domed ceilings in the small interlinking chambers that make up Saint's private lair. Catacombs — refurbished and decorated, but under-ground tombs nonetheless. The walls and ceilings are painted white, as though that somehow disguises the dark, morbid roots of the place. Each one acts as a private room or booth, catering to Saint's much less savoury business acquaintances. This is the rumoured club that draws the people upstairs. And it's right beneath their feet. This place is a who's who of London's underground world. Fitting that they be down here really.

I move through the catacombs until I reach the huge wooden doors at the end. Knocking once, I push it open. I'm early, and I know Saint will hate that, but a petty part of me just loves to wind him up. To watch that little demon in his head throw itself against the bars of its cage and test the limits of that religious restraint he forces upon himself.

The room literally looks like a throne room, and I know it's deliberate. My brother is that unhinged that he genuinely thinks himself like a deity among men. There's a fireplace across the other side of the room. And in the centre is a single chair, the wood intricately carved and the back high: a throne. Across from the chair is a long sofa, so he can hold court, of course.

"Ah, Judas, it's been a while." A figure moves away from a shadowy corner where a small bar sits.

"Jase." My half-brother moves closer, and the warm glow of the fire washes over one side of his face, igniting the copper strands of his messy hair. Jase is my mother's shame, as she likes to say. The love child of one of William's affairs, of which there are many, I'm sure. He doesn't share the same dark hair and blue eyes as Saint, William, and myself, but the apple definitely didn't fall far from the tree. By the time Dad found out about him, Jase was fourteen and had just been arrested for stealing a car.

He and I have never had much reason to get on, but he and Saint are close. Very close. Jase is Saint's right-hand man, and quite possibly the only person he truly trusts. Approaching, he hands me a glass of whiskey, and I take it from him before he moves over to the couch.

"How have you been?" he asks. "How is the abstinent life treating you?" A quick smile flashes over his face, and he looks every inch my father for a moment. I roll my eyes and ignore him. He just laughs. "I have to say. I admire your dedication to the cause. Playing the role, keeping your head down. I can't think of anything worse than banging on about God all day." Again, I say nothing. We aren't friends. We're business acquaintances at best. He nods toward the glass in my hand. "I'd drink that if I were you."

"Where is he?"

Jase checks his watch. "Well, you're early, and you know how he is about his appointments." I do. Saint keeps his appointments exactly. Not a minute before or after. If you're early, and he happens to be here, he will ignore you.

Five minutes later, Saint strolls into the room like royalty returning to the empire. His two bodyguards halt outside, swinging the heavy doors closed behind him. The jazz music from beyond cuts off and the silence that went unnoticed before feels deafening with my brother in the room.

Everything about Saint makes people uncomfortable, even me. He's too still, his gaze too intense, his movements too predatory, because that's exactly what he is; a predator and everyone around him is prey.

He swipes a hand slowly down the front of his immaculately tailored suit, black, of course. His dark hair contrasts against pale skin, making him look like a vampire. He's not far off, seeing as I'm pretty sure he never leaves this cave. Blue eyes, the same shade as my father's stare back at me, but colder, much, much colder.

"Saint."

He turns away from me and goes to his throne, releasing the button of his jacket before he sits. "Brother."

"I know you're pissed off —"

"Pissed off? No, Judas, I'm not pissed off. I'm perplexed." He tilts his head to the side, taking the drink that Jase places in his hand without even looking at him. Jase clears his throat and quietly moves away. When Jase is uncomfortable you know it's about to implode into a smouldering pile of shit. "I'm struggling to comprehend why you test me so."

"It's not —"

"Enough." He holds up his hand and stands. "You blackmail one of my cleaners. By threatening to. Sell. Me. Out," he hisses, a rare flash of temper peeking through that icy veneer. "Do you know what I do to people who threaten me, Judas?"

"I'm aware," I drawl. He's so melodramatic.

His eyes snap to mine. "Our sharing the same blood won't save you if you fuck with what's mine. The only reason you aren't dead already is because Mother would be upset."

"Comforting to know you care."

He looks me up and down. "You are a sinner, Judas, a murderer, a false pretender, a heathen parading as a servant of God. No, I do not care." I want to laugh because Saint is for all intents and purposes, crazy. But he's devout in his religion. The madman with a moral compass? No, Saint simply believes in his final fate so absolutely that he avoids doing anything that might send him to hell. His 'good deeds' and forgiving heart are founded only in the narcissistic need to go to heaven. That's it. Other than that, everyone is beneath him, except my mother of course because my mother is a true believer. My mother is the one that made him this way. Truthfully though, what else could she do? I may be a wrong 'un as she so often tells me, but Saint has the devil in him. He's a psychopath, and I mean that in the absolute clinical sense of the word. So she did the only thing she could. She made him fear God's wrath enough to curb his own nature. Saint is the product of a conflicted conscience, but I never trust him. And as for his sin-free soul, well...he simply racks them up on Jase's instead.

Saint wouldn't kill me, but he'd get Jase to. Or at least try.

"It's a global business for fuck's sake. There's plenty of scope for extra cash." I refuse to tell him exactly why I'm pushed to such extremes.

He moves closer, one slow step at a time. Stalking me. "I'm careful, selective, practised." He accentuates each word. "What I do is art. And you want to come in and run your filthy drug money through my contact?"

"Your money's just as dirty, Saint," I say on a snort. He's so on his high horse about his damn counterfeit money, preaching about how drugs are sinful, and the business is beneath him. Meanwhile, he pours millions of fake cash into an already ailing economy.

"I'm careful," he repeats, looking me over as though I offend him.

"So am I."

"They will follow your little trail of breadcrumbs all the way back to Dawson and in turn me." This is the other aspect to Saint, his paranoia.

"I'll cut you in," I say on a resigned sigh.

He pauses, his lips pressing together. I can see the possibilities firing through his mind at a hundred miles an hour. He'd love it, the idea of making money from my father's empire, the one he refused to be a part of. Saint is not above gloating.

"That does not negate the risk."

"No." I step closer to him, unable to help the smile. "But you're thinking about it, Saint because it's something for nothing. It's a middle finger to Dad and me, and it's a degree of control."

His eyes meet mine, that madness always lingering just below the surface.

"No."

Here we go. "I'll owe you."

He cocks a brow. "*What* will you owe me?"

He knows what I'm going to say because it's the currency we always used as kids, back when I feared hell as much as he does. A slow smile pulls at his lips before I've even spoken the words. "I'll owe you a sin."

His eyes light with the same feral delight that they used to when we were too small to really appreciate the full gravity of what a sin could be used for. Now though...now he knows. Now I know. All too well.

"Done. You owe me a sin." I hold my hand out to him because he always requires a gentleman's handshake on these things. Instead, he simply tilts his head in that unsettling way of his. "But I want it sealed in blood."

I grind my teeth together. "You know that's not how it works."

Jase silently places a knife into Saint's waiting hand, and I release a long breath.

"Think of it as a promise. It's on your skin, so I know you'll honour it."

I glare at him before unfastening the buttons of my shirt and tugging the material open. A delighted grin pulls at his lips as he steps closer to me, placing a cold hand against my chest. Leaning in, he presses the tip of the blade to my skin and drags it downward in a burning trail, a cut about an inch and a half long. I keep my eyes focused on him, and he steps back before waving a hand at Jase who hands me a paper towel. I press it to the cut, soaking up the blood.

"Happy?"

"You're running out of room, brother."

I shrug shirt back in place. "Do we have a deal?"

He simply turns away, waving a hand through the air. "You may leave."

I've done a lot for the family business over the years, but backing Saint Kingsley into a corner is by far the most dangerous.

4

DELILAH

I WAKE up with a pounding headache and my stomach churning like a cement mixer. Blinking my eyes open, I flinch against the dull, late morning light pouring through the open curtains. There's a moment, a perfect moment where I forget, and then the same as every morning for the last month, it all comes crashing back in. All the emotions that I temporarily suppressed with alcohol last night wash over me like a breaking wave. That lead weight that seems to take up residence in my stomach on a daily basis makes an appearance, and the temptation to drink myself unconscious again is more than appealing.

Dragging myself out of bed, I go to the bathroom and glance at my reflection in the mirror. Dark shadows linger beneath my eyes, and my cheekbones protrude sharply against my almost translucent skin. My haggard appearance should probably bother me, but I just don't care.

It's not until I walk downstairs to make some coffee that I see the calendar on the wall. Today's date is circled in thick red pen with stars drawn all around it and the scrawl of Izzy's handwriting. *Izzy's birthday. Buy me cake!* Shit, how long has it been since the funeral? Two weeks? I feel like I've lost two weeks of my life in an alcoholic coma. I've been going through the motions, even going to uni some days. Just drunk. And now today is what would have been Izzy's birthday. She died a month short of twenty-two. If that's not a tragedy, then I don't know what is.

Guilt on top of guilt on top of guilt. I pour a cup of coffee and throw in a good dose of Baileys because being sober does not appeal right now.

"Lila."

I turn at the sound of Tiff's voice. Her eyes trace over my face, her brows pinching together in silent concern. "Hey."

Tiff leans against the far counter and folds her arms over her chest. Her eyes drop to the coffee in my hand before shifting to the bottle on the side. "Izzy wouldn't want you to do this to yourself," she says.

"Well, she's not here to ask, is she?" *And that's on me.* But Tiff doesn't know that. She doesn't know that I gave Izzy's boyfriend those drugs, or in fact that I've ever dealt drugs. No one does. Izzy was the only one I ever told, and only because I knew she'd never disapprove. Izzy was too wild for petty judgements. Tiff is lovely, but she's studying to be a doctor. Sure, she parties and gets drunk sometimes, but she's good. She doesn't get me like Izzy did.

"It was an accident. It's sad and awful, but she's gone. You're still here." Tiff shakes her head. "And you're wasting your life being drunk all the time."

"Thanks, but I just...can't do this today."

Today we absolutely should be drunk all day, because if Izzy were here, she sure as hell would be. Isabelle always threw crazy birthday parties and would go on random day trips. Last year, she decided at midnight that we were going to go to Paris. So we got in the car, and by eight the next morning, we were in Paris. She never thought anything through, just acted. I miss it. I miss her brand of crazy and the way she made me feel a little more normal when I was with her. I miss the way that she never questioned anything. *There are no wrong decisions in life*, she would say.

I take a shower and put on a clean pair of jeans and a jumper. When I look in the mirror, I look more human.

Putting another coffee in a to-go cup, I walk outside. I flinch because it's bright and loud, and my head is still pounding.

On the tube, I watch the people going about their normal lives, and I envy them. I wish I could just go back to normal. I loved Izzy, but I wish I could just forget, that this lead weight would disappear.

By the time I get to uni, the Baileys in my coffee is kicking in a little, bathing me in a layer of blissful numbness.

Taking a seat at the back of the lecture hall, I tuck myself into a corner. The lecturer talks about something, but I have no idea what. I'm like a puppet on strings, going through the motions — feeling nothing, seeing nothing.

After the lecture, I head home, but on the way, I stop in at the off license and the bakery.

The house is quiet when I get in. The sun is just starting to dip, spilling its last rays through the kitchen window.

Removing the cupcake from its little box, I rummage in the junk drawer for a candle and place it in the middle of the pink icing. Striking a match, I light it, watching the little flame dance back and forth happily. Taking the cheap bottle of vodka, I twist the top off with a satisfying crack.

"Here's to you, Izzy. Happy birthday." I lift the bottle before tipping it back, watching the bubbles glug upward as the rancid petrol taste burns down my throat. So, I sit, and drink, and watch the wax drip onto the icing because I don't have the heart to blow that stupid candle out.

I jolt awake at the sound of loud banging. It takes me a moment to work out where I am. It's dark, but moonlight gives enough illumination for me to see I'm in my living room, on the sofa.

Bang, bang, bang. It's the front door. Dragging myself off the sofa, I stumble down the hallway to answer it. When I pull the door open, I find Nate standing there. My heart falters for a beat, and my fingers tighten into fists. The flickering orange glow of the streetlight behind him gives his dark hair a demonic sheen. I haven't seen him since the day of Izzy's funeral, two weeks ago, the day I tried to go to the police. He's texted and called non-stop. Tiff mentioned him turning up here once or twice, but she never let him in.

"What do you want?"

"You didn't call me back," he says, his brows pulled into a tight frown.

A high-pitched laugh slips past my lips. "Seriously?"

"Baby, don't be like that." Stepping closer, he invades my space.

"I can't deal with you right now, Nate."

Placing a finger beneath my chin, he forces me to look at him. "Are you drunk?"

I go to close the door, but he shoulders it open with his body.

"What the fuck, Lila?"

Squeezing my eyes shut, I will my head to stop spinning. "Please leave."

His palms cup my cheeks and warm breath rushes over my lips. "I'm sorry, okay?"

I open my eyes and meet the deep chocolate of his irises. "What for? Threatening me? Or for the friend I killed?"

"You didn't kill her, and I'm just trying to protect you."

"You're protecting yourself," I snap. "She's dead. I'm guilty, and you're just...living your life." All the anger, the frustration, the hurt, it just pours out, streaming down my face in salty wet lines.

Without warning, Nate pulls me close and wraps his arms around me. I know I should hate him, that I should fight this, but I don't. I just accept it because, in my drunken haze, I think I need it. For a single moment, I want to feel as though I'm not entirely alone with this, and seeing as he's the only person who knows what truly happened, he's all I've got. I hear the front door click shut, and then he scoops me up, holding me to his chest as he carries me to my room. I sit on his lap, crying into his shirt until a huge wet patch stains the material.

"It'll all be fine. Just give it time."

"I don't think it can be," I whisper.

There's a pause, and he inhales a deep breath, his chest rising and falling beneath my cheek. "It will."

He hugs me tighter, but it does nothing to fight off the trembling of my body. "All I see is her face. Judging me. Hating me." I press my fingers to my temples. "It never stops."

Grabbing my jaw, he twists my head until I'm forced to look up at him. "This is just the way the world works, Lila. You didn't force the pills down her throat. You don't even know if that was it. She might have taken something else."

I know he's trying to make it better, but he's not. The world exists on the butterfly effect. One person's decisions and actions affect another's. My choice had a consequence.

Nate leaves in the early hours of the morning to handle some 'business'. He guts the house of all the alcohol before he goes, and in doing so, takes my only crutch. I can't sleep, and the more I sober up, the louder my thoughts are getting.

Getting out of bed, I tear through the kitchen, trying to find an errant bottle he forgot about. There must be something, somewhere. Izzy always had a stash... Climbing the stairs, I creep down the hall, the dodgy floorboard at the end squeaking as I move to her door.

Pushing the door open, I suck in a breath and turn the light on. Her parents came and took a lot of her stuff, but the furniture, the made-up bed, the desk...all remain. I swear I can smell the faintest hint of her perfume. Bingo. I snatch the bottle of Tequila off her windowsill, though there's barely a couple of shots worth at the bottom. Of course, not even Nate would come in Isabelle's room to search for booze. No one comes in here. Unscrewing the top, I take a swig as I go to the desk, to the corkboard that hangs above it. Pictures are tacked to it, and buried among them is one of us in Thailand, where we met. We are at a party with both of our straws in the same giant frozen margarita. If only we knew then where our naïve antics would lead.

Taking a seat on the bed, I stare at it through tears, draining the remainder of the bottle. Falling back on the sheets, I lie there. Waiting for my mind to quiet, but it never does. On a groan, I push to my feet and walk out of the room. I need more. Grabbing my purse and coat, I head downstairs and step outside. My goal is the corner shop, a couple of streets over, but when I get there, it's closed. Shit. Somewhere around here must be open. And so I walk, aimlessly, my thoughts drifting until I realise I'm standing in a park. A full moon sits low in the sky, illuminating everything in a muted silvery light. There are flowerbeds full of bright yellow daffodils that seem to glow even in the darkness, as though their symbolic happiness simply cannot be extinguished.

At the edge of the park is an old stone wall, and beyond it lay headstones, scattered through the shadows of the enormous church, every bit as forgotten as the long-dead people buried beneath them. I slip through the tiny gateway and move between the stones, soaking in the utter silence that seems to linger in a graveyard more than any other place. It's as though the world is holding its breath, paying its respects. I trace my fingers over one stone, the top covered in moss and the face so weatherworn that the writing has long since eroded.

Following the graveyard around the church, I find myself standing on the other side, by the main road. The ancient stone steps lead up to solid double doors, and one is open. The hand-painted wooden sign says it's St Mary's Catholic church. I can already smell the incense in the air, and the glow of candlelight from inside acts like a beacon to a lost soul. I linger on the steps for a moment, feeling stupid. And then I remember that Catholics have wine. Without thought, I ascend the steps and go in. It's silent, with not a single person in sight. The air is chilled, the result of a solid stone structure and no heating. But despite that, there's a sense of calm and peace here.

I'm not sure I believe in anything more than what's right in front of us, but there is something to be said for a church. A sense of serenity that could almost make a non-believer feel as though something greater has reached out a hand and offered a safe haven from their demons. Though I have no explanation for it, for the first time in weeks, I feel as though I am not alone in my anguish.

For a moment, I forget why I came in here. Taking a seat on a pew at the front of the church, I glance up at the statue of the Virgin Mary, her open arms, and her tender expression. Maybe she'll understand me.

I jolt awake and groan when my neck screams in protest.

"Sorry, but you can't sleep here," someone says.

"Sorry. I didn't mean to." I blink and focus on the figure standing in front of me. His long black robes make him look like a reaper, but as I lift my eyes, I see the white dog collar at his throat. He's a priest. When I reach his face, I pause. He has the kind of face that could lure even the most righteous into sin. He's beautiful. Not handsome or hot, but truly beautiful.

"You're...the priest?" I ask.

He smiles, and it sinks a dimple into the chiselled plane of his cheek. "The collar would suggest so." Deep blue eyes meet mine, twinkling with amusement. "And the church." He holds his hands out, gesturing to our surroundings.

"Of course." I drop my chin to my chest.

"I'm Father Kavanagh." He takes a seat beside me, and for a moment we just sit in silence. "I've never seen you before. What brings you here?" he asks.

"I'm not religious."

"Alright."

I glance at him. "That's it? Alright?"

A wry smile makes an appearance and something in my chest flutters. "You came here because you're looking for something. You just don't know what it is." His eyes meet mine, and they're so earnest that I feel as though I would trust him with my life.

"I came here looking for wine," I blurt.

He laughs, the sound like thunder rolling through the high arches of the stone church. "That's a new one."

"Do you have any?"

He laughs. "You smell like a distillery. I don't think you need any more."

I push to my feet. "Well, thank you for your holy opinion."

"Sit," he barks, and for some reason, I comply instantly.

"What's your name?"

"Delilah."

His gaze locks with mine, so full of promises, so intense I feel like I could drown in it. "Do you need something to believe in, Delilah?"

"I think I do," I whisper.

5

JUDAS

THERE'S something so tragic about her — vulnerability, desperation. Mahogany hair spills over her shoulders, framing a pale face. Dark circles linger beneath her eyes, the exact colour of storm clouds and so full of sadness I can almost feel her pain. And yet, it makes her obvious beauty become so much more.

"Would you like to confess, Delilah?" I ask. I want to know what haunts this lost little lamb to make her stray so far from the flock.

Her full lips part and then close again. "I can do that?"

"I'm here. You're here. And the confessional is here."

"Is...everything I say confidential?"

"It's between you and God. I'm simply the messenger," I recite the words I've spoken a hundred times before. People want to confess their sins, to buy their way to heaven, but they don't want their dirty little secrets getting out. I'm curious what Delilah has to say that could warrant her asking though. Confidentiality implies shame at best and illegality at worst, and that always excites me.

Offering her my hand, she slides cold fingers over my

palm before I pull her to her feet. I show her to the confessional, and she steps inside. Taking up position, I settle on the hard wooden bench.

"So, you start by crossing yourself. Then say; forgive me, Father, for I have sinned."

She repeats the words back. "Forgive me, father, for I have sinned."

"Then you'd usually say how long it's been since your last confession, but seeing as you aren't religious…"

"I've never confessed," she confirms. A virgin. Full of sins un-forgiven — just languishing on the soul. Religious or not, I find that usually does something to a person. Guilt and absolution are powerful. The human conscience is fragile, and often religion will lend it a false sense of strength when it falters.

"Well, now is the time, Delilah." I lean forward, a small rush firing through my veins. I want to know what she did, more so than usual. Perhaps it's that deep, gut-wrenching sadness I saw running rampant in those eyes of hers. Or maybe it's simply that she's beautiful. Beauty hides a multitude of sins, but scratch the surface, and they come spilling out.

"I…" She pauses and takes a shuddering breath. "I did something horrible, and I can't forgive myself."

"We all do horrible things."

"But it hurt someone else," she says, her voice hitching.

"Did you intend to hurt them?"

"No!"

"But you feel guilt?"

"Yes."

"Then God will forgive if you are truly repentant."

I hear the soft hitch of her breath, a sniffle, and through the divider, I can just make out the porcelain of her cheek, the tears tracking over her skin. I usually like the anonymity of the confessional, to not see the faces of the damned, but I find myself staring, watching a single tear trickle over jaw and down the column of her throat. She's a pretty girl, but she's stunning when she cries.

I listen to people confess how they cheated on their wife or were unkind to their neighbour. Normal people acting in human ways, seeking absolution, just so the pearly white gates are open to them. And I, the false pretender, grant them their salvation, knowing they're not truly sorry for any of it because isn't that the way the world works? Everyone is fundamentally selfish.

But this girl...this girl is different. Tortured.

"You believe in God?" she breathes.

"Of course."

"If you were him, would you forgive me?" Interesting.

"I don't know what you did. He does." There's a beat of silence. "Do you believe you are worthy of redemption?"

"No." Ah, a sinner who does not seek forgiveness, only acceptance. A rare gem.

"Then where does that leave you, Delilah?"

There's a pause. "Lost," she whispers.

"Then find your way home." I stand up. "Goodbye, Delilah."

I leave the confessional, disappointed that she didn't tell me more. That she didn't pour out her soul.

I want to know how far the pretty girl with the sad eyes has fallen.

6

DELILAH

When I get home, I quietly open the front door, letting myself in. The scent of brewing coffee hits me, and when I step into the kitchen, I see Tiff leaning on the breakfast bar reading the paper. She's dressed in workout clothes, and I know she's getting ready to go to her morning yoga class.

She glances up at me, her brows pulling tightly together. "Where have you been?"

"Um...I actually went to a church."

"Church?" I nod. "It's six thirty in the morning."

"I know."

"And you aren't religious."

"I know. I just sort of...ended up there."

"Well, good."

I frown. "Good?"

A small smile touches her lips, but it doesn't reach her eyes. "You look like shit, and you've been drunk for the last month." She shrugs one shoulder. "You need something." I chew my bottom lip, feeling like such a failure because she's right — I'm a mess. "Hey, look, if the church helps...Millions of people turn to faith for guidance. They can't all be wrong."

It's ridiculous because, for the first time since the morning when I heard Izzy was dead, I feel a sense of peace. The church did that for me. *He* did that for me, with his calming voice and his reverent presence.

"Thanks, Tiff. I'm going to try and sleep a little."

I don't manage to sleep, but my mind is a little clearer, and that tiny window through the fog gives me so much hope I could cry. The problem is, I'm terrified of the moment that it clouds again. So I google St. Mary's Church, Hammersmith. It pulls up a website, and I look at the schedule.

A few hours later, I make a to-go coffee, minus the Bailey's, and take the tube to uni. My head is pounding, and I'm not sure if it's from the vodka last night or my sudden cold turkey withdrawal from alcohol after weeks of depending on it. I barely take in anything the lecturer says again, and I can feel myself getting anxious. It's like there's this horrible, dark, sludginess living in me, and it's been temporarily pushed down, but it's rising again. I don't know what to do, but this seems like a reasonable path for now. Surely it has to get better? Just one day at a time. Get through it and move onto the next.

When class is over, I'm practically jogging to the Piccadilly tube station. I don't even go home, just make my way straight to the church. As soon as I set foot inside that building, everything calms. Breathing becomes a little easier, and my heart rate levels out, becoming more regular and steady. There are a couple of people in the pews, their heads bowed in prayer. An older lady lights a candle in front of the statue of the Virgin, crossing herself as she mutters words under her breath.

Seeing the confessional, I make my way over, like a moth to a flame. That tiny little box suddenly feels like my only safe place. I looked on their website, so I know they take confessional between two and five in the afternoon. Stepping inside, I pull the curtain closed. It's only a piece of material, but as soon as it's drawn, the outside world disappears, and everything shrinks. To this wooden booth, to me, and the man on the other side of the partition, to that secret bond we share at this moment. I'm not a believer, but I feel the power in it.

I try to remember what the priest told me to do. Cross myself. "Forgive me, father, for I have sinned," I breathe. "It's been one day since my last confession."

"Go on, child," a rough northern voice says.

It's not him, and gutting disappointment cuts me to my core. I swallow around the sudden lump in my throat, and I don't think I realised just how much I needed this. Not necessarily the church, or even confession, but him. And I don't understand that because he's a stranger. We spoke for no more than half an hour, but he brought me calm. There was something in his eyes that I wholeheartedly believed. When he spoke, he could have been the voice of God himself.

If I confess to this man, will it be the same? I already know the answer. No. Why is that? He was just a priest, the same as the man on the other side of this partition.

"I...I need to go."

Stumbling from the confessional, I walk out of the church without looking back. I leave without my fix, without the forgiveness that I so desperately need.

The next day, I stand just inside the doorway of the church, inhaling the thick spicy smell of the incense. I'm jittery and nervous, and I don't know why. Sunlight spills through the stained-glass windows, lighting a path in front of me like a real holy apparition. It's beautiful, enlightening, uplifting.

My heeled boots click over the uneven stone floor, and my steps falter as I glance at the confessional. It's such an inconspicuous thing, the dark wood of the booth dwarfed by the colossal size of the building it sits in. The heavy green velvet fabric of the curtains has now faded almost to grey, years of sunlight stealing its vibrancy.

Taking a deep breath, I wait until an older lady leaves the booth, and I take her place. Once again, I immerse myself in the quiet, the seclusion, and the overwhelming sense of something other. My heart pounds in my chest, and I'm nervous, but I don't know why.

I cross myself. "Forgive me, father, for I have sinned," I whisper. "It has been two days since my last confession."

"I will hear your confession."

That deep melodic voice washes over my senses like a soothing balm, and I release a breath I hadn't realised I was holding. I almost forget why I even came, as though my purpose was simply to hear his voice.

"I came here the other night, and...you made it better," I say. "You probably don't remember me," I stutter.

"I remember, Delilah." My heart thumps heavily, and I say nothing for long moments until the silence starts to feel oppressive.

"I came yesterday, to confess, but it wasn't you, so..." I stumble awkwardly. "I left."

"I'm glad I could help." I hate that I can't see him, can't judge his reactions.

"You did."

There's a moment of silence and then a low laugh from him. "Are you going to confess?"

"Can I confess the same sin twice?"

"If you do not feel you are truly repentant or forgiven, then yes, you can confess as many times as you like."

"Then I did a horrible thing, and I can't forgive myself."

"God forgives all, Delilah."

I nod to myself and tears prickle against the backs of my eyes. "Even those who don't believe in him?"

"He believes in you." And in those words, I hear that *he* believes in me; the mysterious priest with the disarming smile and a strange calmness to him. For some reason, his belief has so much value.

"Thank you, father."

I stand and open the curtain before leaving the church. I want to turn around and go back. I want to force the priest to tell me it'll be okay because right now he seems to be the only person that can make me feel like it actually will be. Call it a coping mechanism, a fix, a band-aid, but, right now, it's all I have. And this is how I know that I'm truly losing it because I'm turning to a man of a faith I don't even have to help me.

7

JUDAS

"Forgive me, father, for I have sinned. It has been two days since my last confession."

I smile, instantly recognising her voice, soft and well spoken, undoubtedly feminine.

"I will hear your confession," I repeat the words I've probably spoken hundreds if not thousands of times. Mundane words meant as a service to God, but they feel wrong with her. Devoid. I lean forward, tilting my head slightly towards the partition because I don't want to miss a word.

"I did a horrible thing, and I can't forgive myself."

Five days. She's been in here for the last five days like clockwork. I'm not even supposed to be here this afternoon, but I came in. For this. For her. Because in such a short time, she's become an obsession of sorts. She came the last time Father Daniels was taking confession, but she wouldn't confess to him. Only me. And that does something to me. Five days and she always says the same thing. *I did a horrible thing, and I can't forgive myself.* And every day, I give her the same bullshit response, waiting. Patiently waiting for the moment when she spills her dark secrets to me.

Until then, we're both pretending, both playing a role. Maybe she needs that right now, to be the lost lamb, seeking her shepherd. Whatever eats away at her day after day, she never gives it voice, but she will. One day. And oh, how I've come to long for that moment.

Each time she comes here, I'm on edge, waiting, desperate to hear the truth fall from her lips. I want to know what she did. I want to believe that this girl, the pretty girl with the sad eyes, is, in fact, corrupt. As corrupt as me, even? The thought shouldn't be so thrilling.

I press my back to the solid wood behind me, forcing myself to remain there and not lean forward, not to catch just a glimpse of her face.

"God forgives those who truly repent, Delilah," I say, like a broken record. At this point, she usually leaves, but not today.

"I do repent."

No, she doesn't. That's what's so intriguing about her. "Then why do you come here every day?"

"Because I don't want to feel like this."

"Then just stop."

"I can't!"

I smile. "Why do you think people confess, Delilah?"

"To make themselves feel better?"

"No, because if I tell them they're forgiven then it allows them the freedom of a guilt-free conscience."

"But what if I deserve the guilt?" There's nothing I love more than someone who puts themselves on the cross.

"If you think that, then you will continue to carry it."

"I don't know how to change it," she whispers.

"You simply step away from the whipping post, Delilah."

There's a beat of silence then her hand presses up against the divider, the intricate mesh pressing into the milky skin of her palm. The urge to touch her creeps up on me, whispering in my ear what a perfect little sinner she is, how beautiful, how sad.

"Thank you, father," she says before her hand slides away and she leaves the booth.

"I'm off." I glance up from the paperwork in front of me. Father Daniels is lingering in the doorway, a friendly smile on his rosy face. I suspect he hits the wine a little too hard. His greying hair is shaved close to his head, and his dog collar cuts into his pudgy neck. "Are you okay doing that?" He nods towards the papers.

I offer what I hope is a friendly smile. "I'm fine. Good night."

"Night." He shuffles away, and I go back to the papers, which would appear to be the churches work, but is in fact, my own.

This time it's the funding of a school in Puerto Rico, which of course will never actually happen. Running money through a church is like taking candy from a baby as they say. Put money in one end as anonymous donations, it comes out the other as a charitable project with the money going to a blanket company's off-shore account.

My phone rings, the shrill sound echoing around the church office.

"Yeah?"

"Judas, it's Reno." Reno runs one of the street gangs in South London. He moves a lot of product for me, a crucial link in the chain.

"Reno. How are you?" I keep my voice low, just in case.

"Look, I've got to be straight with you, The Italians offered me a deal," he says in his coarse cockney accent. The fucking Moretti family are raping me on a daily basis at the moment.

I pinch the bridge of my nose, biting back a groan. "How much?"

"Ten percent less."

"I'll match it, but keep it quiet."

"Alright." He hangs up, and I slam my fist against the desk. Shit!

I'm getting screwed from multiple angles. First with Fire closing, and I have no idea when the authorities will cut the miles of red tape they've got me wrapped up in. There's a police investigation. It's a mess. The knock-on effect is that several clients then got windy and started buying from the Italians. And now, they're trying to take the remaining clients that I have. There's a reason my family has reigned this city for the last thirty years though. We're strategic, and we're powerful, and someone in the family always has a string they can pull. The problem is, a Kingsley never does something for nothing. Family or not.

Dragging both hands through my hair, I tilt my head back and release a long breath. There's only one person I can ask for help with this, and luckily she owes me a favour.

I dial the number programmed on speed dial and place it to my ear, listening to it ring.

Someone picks up but says nothing. "It's Judas Kingsley. I need to speak to Myrina," I say. The line cuts off, and I wait.

My entire family is crazy and paranoid, but it's what keeps them, us, at the top of the food chain.

Myrina Kingsley is, to the outside world, the woman

everyone wants to either be or have: beautiful, charming, and wealthy. That side of the family own half of London: hotels, nightclubs, bars, restaurants, and property. Myrina even owns a fifty-one percent share in a pharmaceutical company, so she can provide cheap medicine to her charity, which aids third world countries. To everyone looking in, she's the sweet heiress using her family's money to make the world a better place. Little do they know...Myrina Kingsley is a force of nature disguised as a rainbow. A drug lord. The daughter of Richard Kingsley, former drug lord and now mayoral electorate. How times change. Either way, Myrina needs only make a phone call to Uncle Rick, and he'll do whatever she wants. Including getting my club re-opened.

My burner rings with an unknown number, and I answer it.

"Hello?"

"Judas, it's been a minute," my cousin purrs, and I can imagine the sensual curve of her lips, and her twisting a piece of her long blonde hair around her finger as she speaks. She can't help it, she's been raised to use everything at her disposal to get what she wants, and she does. There's the sudden sound of loud music before it cuts off again. It's Friday night, so she'll be at her nightclub in Soho: Suave. It's one of the hottest clubs in the city of course. Nothing less would do.

"I need a favour, Myrina."

She lets out a small laugh. "Of course you do."

"I wouldn't ask if it wasn't necessary."

"It must be bad if you're coming to me. You and Saint still not kissed and made up?"

"Saint doesn't owe me a favour."

There's a beat of silence, the acknowledgement of our

shared, dark secret. I have never asked Myrina for anything, and we both know she owes me ten times over.

"What do you need?" she asks, all traces of the joking girl disappearing, replaced by the ruthless businesswoman she really is, the daughter of a crime boss. A Kingsley.

"Fire; up and running as soon as possible. I know you can pull strings."

"And what are you going to do for me?"

"I thought I just made that clear. You owe me. Five years to be exact."

"I never asked you for a thing, Judas," she snaps. No, she didn't. I never intended to use this against her, but I know Myrina. She trades in blood and favours.

"Then call it a freebie to your favourite cousin."

"Well, if I hand out favours to you, then I'll have to do it for everyone. Then I look weak, and people ask questions." There's a pause. "You promised me, Judas."

"I'm not breaking that promise. Just pull some strings."

"Fine, but I am going to need something in return. You know I'll have to go to Daddy, and he'll ask."

"What do you want?" I sigh, tiring of Myrina's endless games.

She laughs, the tinkling high notes like wind chimes catching on the breeze. "Ten percent. He knows I only act in my own interest, so...ten percent of Fire." She pauses, releasing a long breath. "Remember, I have a reputation to uphold." A reputation as a stone-cold bitch. My baby cousin isn't the fragile teenage girl she once was.

"Five."

"Seven and a half. I'm letting you off lightly because it's not in my nature to screw a man of God."

"Five, and I won't tell your father that you lost your virginity to your teacher." When she was fifteen.

She gasps. "You wouldn't."

"Desperate times, Myrina."

"Fine. Five."

"Fine, and you're not using it as a cleaner."

She snorts. "I'll settle for just taking your stuff," she drawls. The last thing she needs is more property. "Well, as always Judas, it's a pleasure. Watch your back," she drops as a final threat before hanging up.

8

DELILAH

TIFF COMES in and chucks her bag down next to the sofa before collapsing into the cushions. Her blonde hair is falling out of a ponytail, and she looks stressed.

"God, that was a horrible lecture."

"Social sciences?"

She rolls her eyes. "Of course. I'm ordering pizza. Want some?"

"Sure."

She takes out her phone and starts tapping away on the screen. I hear the front door click open and slam shut again, before Summer and a girl I don't recognise walk in.

"This is Trisha," Summer says, her voice stooped low. "Trisha, this is Tiffany and Delilah." Trisha nervously shoves her glasses up her nose, hunching her shoulders. Dark corkscrew curls spill out of her head, and she's wearing a t-shirt with Yoda on the front.

"Hey." I offer her a small wave and Tiff smiles, but her eyes dart towards me. Then I notice Summer flashing me fleeting glances. There's a tension in the air. "What's going on?" I ask.

It's Tiff who steps forward, rubbing her hand over the back of her neck. "Look, Lila, we're struggling to make up the rent…"

Oh my god. "You're replacing her," I whisper.

They both visibly flinch. "It's not like that," Tiff pipes up.

"She was your cousin," I snap at Summer. "How can you just…replace her?"

"You act like you're the only one who cared about her, Delilah! Like we're bad people for going on with our lives. Would you rather we just rack ourselves up in debt?"

"Summer," Tiff tries to interrupt.

"Oh no, that's right, you haven't been paying the extra rent because you've been so busy getting drunk and falling apart."

I glance from Tiff to Summer and finally to Trisha who looks mortified.

"Delilah." Tiff places her hand on my arm.

They're replacing her. Why does that bother me so much? I mean, it's logical and rational. The room is empty. But it shouldn't be, should it?

My phone rings. Nate's name flashes on the screen, and bile creeps up the back of my throat. It's all too much at once, and I feel like I can't breathe. I need air.

Pushing to my feet, I grab my coat and hurry to the front door.

"Where are you going?" Tiff calls after me.

I don't answer. I just need to get out of here.

I don't even remember how I got here. I think my brain just blacked out, on autopilot, until the soothing scent of incense hit me. Finally, I take what feels like my first real lungful of air. I know he might not be here. I want to call out for him, but I realise that I don't even know his actual name.

And calling him Father Kavanagh just feels...I don't know, wrong?

I walk down the centre aisle and pause, staring at the statue of the virgin. I wonder how many people have stood on this exact spot feeling as though everything is so pointless. I wonder how many people have found peace in the serenity of her gaze, in the kindness of her open arms.

The little rack of candles sits in front of her, some lit and some burnt almost to their base. Each one a prayer, a wish, a hope. I take a fresh one and use the stick to light it. And in my mind, I pray for Isabelle's family, that they can find peace. I hope that if there is a life beyond this one, that she finds peace there too.

"Delilah." I turn at the deep rumble of my name on his tongue. Those sapphire blue eyes lock with mine, and a warm sensation spreads through my chest like being immersed in a hot bath. The candlelight dances against his skin and catches on his coal black hair. "Are you alright?" His brows are pinched in concern, and I don't know what to say because I'm not alright. I shake my head. "Come and sit."

He sits on the front pew, and I take the seat next to him. For long moments we say nothing, and I simply stare at the Virgin.

"What's your name?" I ask. He says nothing, and I look at him. "I've come here many times now, and you know my name, but I don't know yours."

He stares at his hands folded in his lap. "Judas."

"Judas?" He's a priest, and he's called Judas.

He nods. There's another long silence before he lets out a sigh. "Why are you here tonight, Delilah?"

We stare at each other for a few seconds, and something physically shifts. My heart skips over itself and my stomach knots tightly. The air crackles between us as if the Virgin were covering her eyes and the Lord himself were holding his breath. "I needed to see you." I breathe the words like a confession.

"I see, well...I was just about to head home." He pushes to his feet and disappointment sinks in my gut. "I was going to stop for sushi. Care to join me?" He holds out his hand.

I tuck my chin to my chest, hiding the small smile. "Yes." My fingers slide over the warmth of his palm and static tears over my skin, making me flush with goosebumps.

Judas disappears out the back for a moment, and when he comes back, he's wearing a black wool coat and suit trousers. He looks...very unholy, and I never realised how much those robes did to hide just how attractive he is.

Neither of us says anything as we move along the damp pavements, walking side by side. When we reach the sushi bar, he opens the door for me and ushers me inside. We take a seat at the bar, and a conveyer belt of dishes in little plastic domes whir around in front of us.

A waitress comes over just as he slides his coat off, revealing a black, buttoned shirt that clings to muscles I didn't expect him to have. The white collar is absent, and I wonder if that means he's 'off duty'. Do priests ever really go off duty? Don't they say God is always watching?

"I'll have a whiskey, and..." He lifts a brow at me.

"Uh, just water please." She leaves, and I prop an elbow on the bar. "I thought priests didn't drink."

He grins. "You're aware the Catholic Church hands out free wine on a Sunday?"

I smirk. "Like happy hour without the three a.m. vomiting?"

"Hmm. The very reason you ever came to the church."

"Not my finest moment."

He laughs, twisting in his seat and resting one elbow casually on the bar. His eyes meet mine for a beat, and I feel like he sees all my dirty secrets. All the parts of myself I wish I could hide and forget about.

"And yet you came back."

"Well, there was a very nice priest there."

"You aren't religious."

My lips pull into a wry smile. "Yeah, but he's not the usual religious type."

"Oh?"

"No, he spares me the bible-bashing bullshit."

The waitress brings our drinks, and he picks his up, swirling it around and sending the ice clinking against the glass.

"Are you sure that's all it is?" he asks, resuming our conversation. "The sparing of bullshit?"

The smile that flashes over his face catches me off guard. Unholy indeed. "He does have a nice voice. Helps when you can't see him in the confessional." I shrug one shoulder and lean in closer. "Probably for the best. He's not a looker."

He chuckles into his drink, and I take a sip of water. "In my experience, most Catholic priests look like paedos."

I laugh and slap a hand over my mouth as water sprays through my lips. I'm coughing and mopping up the mess with a napkin. He simply slaps my back, and when I glance at him, a wicked smirk plays over his lips.

When I can finally breathe again, he asks, "So, why did you come to the church tonight? You weren't looking for wine."

I suck in a deep breath and hold it for a beat. "To see you." When I look up, his eyes are right there, waiting for me. There's something in them that makes butterflies erupt in my chest.

His lips quirk. "But you don't want to talk about it..." I don't want to talk about my problems. I came to him to forget them — because he distracts me. His face, his voice, this little thrill of energy I get when I'm near him; when I'm here, it's all I feel. I don't do well with people. I don't connect with them well, and yet I feel inexplicably drawn to this man. I know I'm safe with him.

"No. I don't want to talk about it."

His index finger taps over his bottom lip absently, and I wonder if he's even aware of the action. Finally, he drops his hand, as though he's finished deliberating. "Then why come?"

"Maybe I don't need to talk. Maybe I just want to...be."

"Okay." He straightens in his seat, moving away from me slightly, and until that point, I hadn't realised that we were both leaning in.

There are a few moments of silence, and then he glances at me. "You done with your 'being' yet?" A cheeky smile flashes over his lips, and I swat his arm. "Come on, tell me some mundane bullshit. What do you do for work?"

"I'm a student."

"Okay. Which university?"

"Kings."

"What do you study?"

"Philosophy." I wrinkle my nose, and he laughs.

"Did you just not know what to do, or..."

"I did a year of medical sciences, and always wanted to be a doctor. Then, I don't know. I guess I just got tired of other people's expectations. And I wanted to piss my Dad off. I temporarily debated becoming a stripper instead, but turns out the long-term career prospects aren't so great." I shrug one shoulder, and he laughs, the sound rumbling over me. "At this stage, I'm pretty sure he'd rather I was a stripper."

"That bad?"

"Yep. So, did you always want to be a priest?"

He huffs a laugh. "I fell into it. Religious mother. Seemed like the easy option at the time."

"You're not...how I imagined a priest would be."

"No? Am I doing it wrong?" He leans closer, and our arms are so near I can feel the heat from his skin.

"No. You're not doing it wrong," I breathe.

He picks up his drink and takes a slow sip, his full lips pressing against the rim of the glass and his Adam's apple bobbing as he swallows. There's a pause, that crackling in the air, and then he places the glass down. "Good," he says, but I've forgotten what we were talking about.

And that's how our evening goes. We talk about the inconsequential details that make up a person's life, and I absorb every crumb of knowledge about him. We eat sushi. He drinks a few glasses of whisky, and that low buzz that seems to permeate the air when I'm near him becomes more incessant as the minutes tick past. I shouldn't like it. I shouldn't indulge in it, but for the time that I'm with him, I forget. It's simply this mysterious man and me. Nothing else. Life has narrowed to this single moment.

When the meal is over, I drop a twenty-pound note on the counter, and he shoves it back towards me before giving the waitress his card.

"Thank you," I say, feeling heat creep into my cheeks.

"The least I can do is feed a starving student." He flashes me a smile. "Besides, you know what they say about the Catholic Church having too much money."

"I hear all the priests are corrupt too."

His smile widens. "Oh, you have no idea."

I follow him outside and the chilly night air meets the warm skin of my cheeks, making them tingle.

"Thank you. I came to the church because something shitty happened, and...you made it better. You always make it better," I murmur.

There's a pregnant pause and his lips part as though he were going to say something but then close again. "Come to Mass tomorrow."

"Mass? Don't you actually have to be a Catholic to attend Mass?"

"I won't tell if you don't." He winks. "Goodnight, Delilah."

Stepping close, his hand slides across my waist and his lips brush against my cheek, lingering just a beat too long before he releases me and turns away, disappearing into the shadows of the night. My heart flip-flops around in my chest, and I close my eyes, inhaling a deep breath of the air that still smells of his cologne. My cheek feels scorched where his lips touched me.

What am I doing?

9

JUDAS

I STAND at the entrance to the church, a smile forced on my face as the regular parishioner's flock to their weekly ritual mass. They all smile, drop money in the donation box, bring cakes and baked bread. This is where my façade is truly tested.

Each week is like a crowning performance, to make a church full of people believe that I am their own personal messenger of God. To make them think that I am a good man, worthy of the adoration I see in their eyes when they speak to me because of course, I am the best of them. A devout man. A lie.

They file in, putting on acts of their own, pretending that they're every bit as holy as the farce I put on.

I greet them one by one, but my smile falters when I spot Angela Dawson. My eyes dart around, looking for her husband, but he's nowhere to be seen. She hasn't come here for weeks, not since the deal we made with Harold. I imagine he warned her away from the corrupt priest, but little does he know... He never did ask how I got those figures. Figures kept on his own personal computer. In his house. She flashes a wide smile at me, and I groan because I do not want to deal with this. It requires a degree of tact because she has no idea of exactly who I am, or just how much I used her. If Harold were to find out that I banged his wife, well...my carefully constructed house of cards could all come tumbling down. A man who has lost his dignity is one thing but add into the equation a woman scorned...no thanks.

She makes her way forward until she's standing in front of me. Her blonde hair is swept into a French twist, accentuating the sharp cheekbones of her face. She's at least twenty years older than me, but her husband's dirty money has been well spent on keeping her immaculately preserved.

"Judas," she says, sliding her hand into mine, but we don't shake. She simply leaves it there until I have to pull away from her.

"Angela. I'm surprised to see you."

She glances over her shoulder, offering a small polite smile to a woman standing nearby. "Yes, I was afraid that Harold had found out. I am sorry. I wanted to see you though." Her lips press together, and she looks genuinely apologetic. Christ.

"Best that you don't." I paint what I hope looks like regret on my face.

She nods and moves on, walking into the church.

I don't need this today.

Once everyone is seated, I take up my position at the pulpit. Every eye is on me, but mine scan the room, looking for one person. The silence is interrupted by the heavy squeal of the church door hinges, and then a small figure slips through the gap.

Delilah.

She's wearing a yellow dress that clings to her small

waist but flicks out over her hips. She looks innocent like sunshine, yet sinful. So damn sinful. Her eyes meet mine, the stormy grey of her irises surrounded by thick lashes. She nervously drags her fingers through the dark waves of her hair before she tiptoes along the length of the back pew. There's no seating left at the back, but instead of walking further into the church, she simply stands against the wall, and I wish she hadn't, because I can see her clear as day. She's all I see, and I can't stop looking at my little sinner, the black lamb of the flock.

This is my moment, the time when I have to try my hardest to play the man these people think I am. The man she thinks I am. But the problem is, when I'm around her, I just want to be myself. To let it all out and see if my suspicions are correct and, if deep down, we're on a level.

Tearing my attention from her, I cross myself. "The Lord be with you."

I read the prayers and recite from the marked bible pages in front of me, though I barely register my own words. People nod, and stare, rapt by the words of the holy book, determined to live their lives by it for the next week. I go through the motions of mass, which I could recite with my eyes closed.

Then comes the communion. Father Daniels stands a few feet away from me with his tray of wine all poured into plastic shot glasses. I usually do the wine because I can't think of anything worse than putting food into people's mouths, but today is different. Today I snatch the bread tray before he can say a word.

I patiently wait for people to approach one by one and drop to their knees in front of the altar. I give them the bread, being careful not to touch anyone. Eventually, Angela approaches, and in my periphery, I see the bright yellow of Delilah's dress only a few people away.

Angela drops to her knees. A small, knowing smile pulling at her lips.

"The body of Christ," I say, and she parts her lips. I practically slam-dunk the piece of bread, refusing to touch her. I can see from the look in her eyes that she's confused. She thinks I want her, that we share a forbidden lust of some kind, hindered only by her husband.

"Amen," she says.

Under pressure from the mounting line, she gets up and moves along to Father Daniels.

A few more people and then Delilah moves in front of me, fidgeting nervously. She waited until the very end, and she's the last person. A shy smile pulls at her lips.

"I don't really know what I'm doing," she whispers.

"Get on your knees," I say, and she does immediately. I fight the groan that lingers in the back of my throat and force myself not to picture her with my dick in her mouth, worshipping me like a good little disciple. Her eyes fix on me, peering through those long, dark lashes, and I know she knows what she's doing. Beneath that façade of innocence, she's a wicked little thing. A temptress.

Clearing my throat, I say the words. "The body of Christ."

I hold up the piece of bread, and she eyes it before her gaze meets mine once more. And that's where it remains as she parts her full lips, waiting. I place the bread on her tongue but hesitate before I withdraw my fingers. She closes her mouth, her lips brushing my fingertips in a feather-light caress, and then her tongue swipes over her bottom lip, catching my thumb.

My pulse shoots through the roof, and a breath hisses

through my lips. There's a pause where neither of us reacts. As though we both forget who we're supposed to be for a moment. I'm supposed to act as though that was clearly a mistake and it doesn't make me want to fuck her on the cold hard floor of the church. But it does. Everything about her does.

Her eyes shift, the settled grey of an autumn sky turning into a churning chaotic storm with lashing rains and rolling thunder. Electricity lingers in the air, and it feels dangerous, as though one spark could set everything off. Poor little lamb, so hungry, and yet she has no idea who or what she's actually dealing with.

"Now you say Amen," I whisper.

"Amen," she repeats before pushing to her feet. The second she breaks eye contact, my body sags, and she takes that static tension with her, allowing me to think clearly once again. She's not the only one affected here, and that's... troubling. I realise that the rest of the congregation are seated, watching me, waiting for me to tie up the service. Shit.

After Mass, I see everyone outside, but I never spot Delilah. She must have slipped away. I go to the office and change out of the white Sunday robes. One second I'm alone, and then like an apparition, as I pull the material over my head, Angela appears. I glare at her before I turn my back and hang up the robes.

"What do you want, Angela?"

"To see you." I take a seat behind the desk, and she moves closer, tugging her blouse down just a little to expose her cleavage. Gone is the put together woman who stands in church, playing the pillar of the community, the Stepford wife. "I know you're angry with me, but it was too risky. Harold's been...distracted. I thought for sure he knew."

"You shouldn't be here."

Her face falls, and her shoulders stiffen. "I thought you'd be happy to see me."

My mind whirs through all the words I can say other than fuck off. The last thing I need is for her to get pissed, and get me struck off, or worse tell Harold. Now, of all times, I need him on board.

Dropping my head forward, I let out a sigh. "Angela." I scrub a hand over my jaw. "Please just go."

"Why?" she snaps.

"Because it's for the best. You are married. You simply need to seek forgiveness and live a pure life."

I look at her, and her lips press tightly together. "You are far from pure, Judas."

"I know, and to my shame. I broke my vows and betrayed God himself. I was tempted, much as Adam was with the apple." I allow my eyes to roam over her body. "I cannot allow it to happen again. So please, do not place yourself in my path. I will not stray again, and I do not wish to hurt you."

I see the indecision, the faltering of her movement. "I'm...I'm sorry."

I nod. "I'm sorry. I should have been stronger. It was wrong of me."

She buys it, and because I know how women like Angela work, I know she's preening that she managed to tempt a man of God to stray. Good. Let her have her moment and leave with her ego intact and her mouth firmly shut.

She takes a tentative step forward and then hesitates. *Just turn around.* She finally turns on her heel, lingering in the doorway for a second. "Goodbye, Judas."

"Goodbye, Angela."

Thank fuck for that. The only saving grace here is that my Ma didn't turn up for mass this week.

When I walk back into the main church, I spot Delilah sitting in the front pew, a copy of the bible in her hands and a frown on her face as she reads the pages. She stayed.

"That bad, huh?"

Her head snaps up, and a blush creeps over her cheeks. "I was just…"

"Reading up?"

"Something like that." She pushes to her feet and smooths the bright yellow fabric of her dress over her thighs. "Walk with me?" she asks, her expression so expectant.

I almost smile. Tsk tsk, sweet Delilah. Crossing lines. But I don't want to walk with her, or do dinner, or play the nice priest. I want her sin, and the more I put that smile on her pretty face, the further she gets from it.

"I have work to do. Sorry." The smile falls.

Her head tilts to the side, stormy grey eyes staring into me in a way that's nothing short of unnerving. I wonder if she sees all the dark parts of herself there. "It's Sunday. Isn't it supposed to be the day of rest?" She's got me there. "Come on. I'll even buy you an ice cream in the park."

My eyes stray to her lips, and now all I can think about is her eating ice cream, licking it. Shit. "Okay," I agree. Not like I didn't believe it before, but I'm definitely going to hell. Here I am, playing the good preacher, acting like I want to help this girl, when in fact I just want to expose all the darkness in her. I want to see her on her knees for me. I want to fuck her and ruin her. She has no idea, like a lamb standing in front of a lion just begging him to eat her. And how is she to know, when the lion looks like a kind shepherd?

She heads towards the church doors, and I walk beside

her. As soon as I step outside, the bright sunshine plays over my skin, warm and inviting. I close my eyes for a second and a luminescent glow forms behind my lids. The scent of fresh cut grass and bonfire catches on the wind, and I inhale it deep into my lungs. The hum of London traffic intermingles with the sound of birds chirping and children playing.

I descend the steps, and she leads the way around the side of the church, through the graveyard and out the little side gate that leads into the park. Flowerbeds bloom with colourful flowers and little daisies pop through the cut grass. Delilah bends down and picks one, twirling it through her fingers as she walks.

"I liked your service," she says.

"You did?" I honestly can barely remember what it was about now. Temptation? God testing us? If I didn't know any better, I'd say he was testing me right now.

"It was...enlightening."

"No, it wasn't. You were bored most of the time."

Amusement pulls at her features. "I used to go to a Church of England. My grandma dragged me when I was a kid. Honestly, I don't remember their service ever being so long."

I laugh. "Catholics like to make a song and dance about everything. You should see a Catholic funeral. It's shit."

We walk across the park to where a little ice cream van sits tucked beneath the branches of a willow tree. A small stream lies just beyond, and a couple of kids are perched on the edge with fishing nets.

Dropping to the grass, I wait while Delilah buys a couple of ice cream cones and comes back, handing me one. She sits next to me, her legs folded to one side and the skirt of her dress fanning over the grass.

And so we sit, and eat ice cream, and watch the world

pass on by. People walk dogs, children play, couples walk hand in hand. It's so...normal. And I have to wonder if this is what people do with their time.

I glance at her in time to watch her reach out and catch an errant drip of ice cream with the tip of her finger. She brings it to her mouth and my cock leaps in my trousers. I inhale a deep breath, willing myself to look away from her mouth.

I'm pretty sure she could tempt a saint, and I'm no saint.

10

DELILAH

THE SUNLIGHT SEEMS to soak into his exposed skin, giving it a golden hue. He glances down at the ice cream in his hand, his lashes shadowing across defined cheekbones. My heart thuds awkwardly as I force myself not to stare at him. He's beautiful. I often think Judas looks more like art than reality, one of Michelangelo's sculptures come to life. An angel barely disguised, put here to lure silly girls like me into temptation. Never has he fit that mould more than when he was standing up on that pulpit, preaching the word of God to his congregation. I could have heard a pin drop, so rapt were they by the words spilling from his perfect lips. I find myself wanting to know him, wanting him to gift me little pieces of his life. There's something about him, a mysterious edge that leads me to believe there's so much more to him than that dog collar.

A fat drop of ice cream melts and trickles down the side of my cone. I catch it with my finger and bring it to my mouth, sucking the sugary goodness from it. I glance at Judas, but pause, my finger still between my lips. In a heartbeat, everything changes. His eyes darken, fixing on my mouth like a predator would with wounded prey. My chest tightens, and my breath hitches as something twisted and forbidden unfurls between us, whispering sordid promises in my ear. We stare at each other for a beat, before I slowly pull my finger from my mouth.

"Judas?" I ask because I don't know what is happening. He's gone very still, and his nostrils flare as his jaw ticks.

"You should stay away from me, Delilah."

I frown, an unexpected stab of pain taking up residence behind my ribs. "What?" I whisper.

"I will only say this once, so hear me when I say that I'm not the man to save you from your sins."

I tense. "You're wrong. You're saving me right now."

Our eyes crash, and suddenly there's not enough air in the world to fill my lungs. He shifts closer, and I lean in, seeking him out like a homing beacon. He's like an open fire on the coldest of days, and I want him to burn me. We get close, so close. I can feel the heat of his breath on my face, and smell the citrus scent of his cologne, with just an undertone of incense.

"Damn it, Delilah," he says under his breath. His fists clench and the corded muscles in his neck strain.

My heart hammers, breaths coming in rapid pants. Everything in me locks down in trembling anticipation because I want to feel his lips on mine. I want him to make me feel safe and warm, and like maybe I'm not truly a horrible person because Judas wouldn't kiss a horrible person, would he?

He doesn't move any closer.

Or maybe I have this all wrong. Perhaps he does think I'm awful. He didn't really want to walk with me, but he's a good man. A kind man. He's a priest. He took a vow. Like a slap around the face, that cold dose of reality pulls me back from the brink. Straightening, I pull away and clear my throat.

"I uh...I have to go." Pushing to my feet, I drop the remainder of my ice cream into a nearby bin before braving a look at him. "But thank you. For walking with me."

He watches me through narrowed eyes, offering me a brief nod before I turn and walk away. What was I thinking?

I step into the house, and my spine stiffens the second I hear the sound of Nate's voice. What is he doing here? I round the hallway into the kitchen and Summer cuts off her awful giggle and looks at me like she's just been caught doing something she shouldn't. Her hand is on his arm, but he's making no effort to touch her. She retracts her hand and steps back, causing me to roll my eyes.

"Lila," Nate says.

"Nate."

His eyes take a slow cruise down the length of my body the same way they always do: arrogant, lazy, and completely sensual. It was that same look that first made me want to tumble headfirst into his bed without a care for the consequences. Now, it just makes me uncomfortable.

"You look good," he says, his teeth scraping over his bottom lip.

Nodding awkwardly, I jerk my head towards the front door and leave the room. Stepping outside, I wait for him to follow and pull the door closed. He shifts closer, and the scent of his leather jacket with a hint of smoke wraps around me, but for once I don't find it settling. I want citrus and incense. I crave something pure and untainted.

"Where have you been, Lila?"

"I..."

"You don't answer my calls. I've been patient, but I don't like having to chase you down." He pulls back, his gaze meeting mine. I can see the anger swirling in his irises. "You know I don't chase, baby."

Placing a hand on his chest, I try to push him away and force a little more space between us. There's something about him, and an alarm is ringing in my head, telling me to tread carefully.

"I told you. I need time."

"Time for what?"

"Time to fucking grieve! Time to...deal with this," I hiss.

His jaw tenses, and I watch the muscles flutter and pulse beneath the surface. "You can't talk to anyone about this."

"I know."

"Summer said you've been going to a church."

"Summer needs to mind her own business," I snap. "And so do you."

He rakes a hand through his hair. The fading sunlight peeks over the top of the house across the street, painting him in a warm glow. Everything about Nate screams bad, and for the first time in my life of questionable men, I don't want it.

"Talk to me, Lila," he says quietly. When his eyes meet mine, they're surprisingly earnest. "You can talk to me."

"No, I can't, Nate because you don't care." He says nothing, and I huff a humourless laugh. "I have to live in that house every day." I jab a finger towards the door. "With people who loved her. *I* loved her. She was the probably the best friend I've ever had."

"You don't have friends, Lila."

Without thought, I pull my arm back and slap him. "Fuck you, Nate." His head whips to the side.

There's a pause, and I take a slow step back because I'm

not sure what he'll do now. He tilts his face towards the sky and closes his eyes, clenching and releasing his fists. "You're upset, so I'll let that go," he grates out.

I wrap my arms around myself. "You were being a dick," I mumble.

"Okay, I'm sorry. I get it. You feel bad."

"No, I don't 'feel bad'. I feel like my life has been going to shit, and where have you been?" God, I hate him. He reminds me of everything that's wrong, but he's also my only solace because he knows. When I'm with Nate, it's the only time I'm not alone with this nasty ugly secret.

He cups my face in both hands, but there's a roughness to his touch. A sick feeling settles in my gut. "I have tried with you, Lila. Don't blame me because you've pushed me out. I'm worried about you, okay? I love you."

It takes a second for the words to sink in, and then I frown, slowly looking at him. "You... Now, Nate? You're going to say that to me now?" I slap his chest and anger bubbles until I feel like I'm brimming with it.

A smug smirk works over his lips, and I want to punch him. "I can feel you slipping, baby. But you're mine. I need you to know it."

Insane. This is insane. I can't do this. I squeeze my eyes shut and count to ten, but it doesn't work. Tears slip past my closed lids, and my chest tightens to the point that I'm waiting for it just to crack open and let all this ugly dark ooze spill out of me. My life is a joke. I've lost all sight of whoever I might have once been, and she was lost to begin with. I feel like an imposter just going through the motions.

"You should go."

Nate's fingers trail over my cheek. "Lila..."

"Go, Nate!" He stills, and his hand falls, his expression morphing from the caring boyfriend to pure anger.

His jaw clenches and his pulse leaps at his throat. I take a wary step back, but he simply jerks his chin in a nod and walks away. I release a long breath and fall back against the front door. I don't need this. Opening the door, I go straight upstairs and collapse on my bed. Exhaustion creeps up on me the same way it always does these days because I can never sleep anymore. My eyelids grow heavy, and I close them for a moment.

I'm in the confessional box. I know it from the distinctive scent of wood polish and old moth-eaten material that's hoarding a lifetime's worth of dust. Slowly, my eyes adjust to the darkness, and I realise I'm not alone in the tiny space. I can feel the heat of another body. The subtle smell of citrus and incense slowly filter through until it dominates everything else. Stark blue eyes become visible in the darkness, so beautiful that they steal my breath.

"Judas."

The confessional is cramped, but he stands with his back pressed to the farthest wall, leaving a foot of space between us. Without even permitting my legs to move, I find myself closing that gap. He looks down at me but says nothing. Then slowly, he reaches up, stroking one knuckle over my cheek.

"So pretty," he whispers. "So steeped in sin." His soft touch becomes a bruising grip around my jaw, and he twists my head violently to the side, forcing me to face the intricate mesh partition. I can see nothing but darkness, yet my heartbeat ratchets higher and higher because it knows something is coming.

Something slams against the divider like a caged animal trying to escape. All I see is red hair, long and tangled, and then she lifts her head, and I see Isabelle's pale, blue-tinged face. Her eyes are completely black. Her lips pulled into a sneer.

"You," she hisses.

A scream slips from my throat, and I clutch at Judas, but he pushes me away. "You," he repeats.

I jolt awake and sit bolt upright, trying to suck much-needed air into my lungs. Sweat clings to my skin, and as the cool air meets it, I shiver.

Crawling from my bed, I find a hoody and tug it on. I manage to find a bottle of wine in the kitchen, so I pour a glass, and then I go to the couch in the living room, turning the TV on to some awful late night show that nobody watches.

It's at this time, between night and morning, where you can truly feel as though you are the only person in the world. The silence, the utter absence of life; it's almost unsettling, and yet I always used to find a certain peace within it. Izzy always said it was the best time of day, that lingering moment where one day is over but another hasn't quite begun. The number of times we've left a party drunk and instead of going home, we've gone somewhere, just to watch the night turn into the first grey tones of dawn.

But now, it feels as though the entire world is buried in sleep, while I sit here, wide-awake, plagued my conscience. There's no peace in my solitude because it feels like I'm always alone now. I'm imprisoned within my own personal cage, yet to the outside world, I look perfectly free. I glance down at my own hands wrapped around the wine glass, and I wonder how they aren't stained red, tinged with blood.

Round and round the thoughts go until I'm two and a half glasses of wine into the bottle, and they start to quiet.

Taking my phone, I scroll through my contacts and call my Mum. I know it's late, or early...I'm not sure. She barely answers the phone at sociable hours, so I'm not surprised when I get her voicemail.

"Hi, this is Lydia Thomas. Please leave a message, and I'll get back to you."

There's a beep, and for a second I just clutch the phone in my hand. "Hey, Mum. It's me. I uh…call me."

I hang up and press my forehead to my knees. Yes, completely alone.

11

JUDAS

I SHOULD BE FOCUSED on my ailing business, but instead, I sit here thinking of nothing but her. I scowl at the walls of the depressing church office, my phone in hand. It's been four days since I've seen her. Since she ran away from me in the park. Since I let her run. She hasn't been to the church, hasn't come to confession. What if she's in another church, confessing to another priest? What if she's telling someone else all her dirty sins?

No. I fire off a text to Jase.

Me: I need you to find someone for me. Name: Delilah. Attends King's College. Philosophy student.

Jase may work for my brother, but he's not averse to a little cash on the side. He can find anyone, anywhere, mainly because Saint has bought him into almost any government network. But he can also hack cameras, phones, computers...

Not even five minutes later my phone pings.

. . .

Jase: Delilah Thomas. Address: 39 Elizabeth Road, Hammersmith. No known employment. Usual fee.

I send him the money and push to my feet, a little thrill of excitement lighting my veins. Removing the dog collar, I slip my black coat on before picking up my car keys.

Delilah's house is a five-minute drive, but as I turn into her street, I spot a familiar figure on the pavement. I pull over and cut the engine, plunging the car into darkness. She makes her way down the road, the streetlights illuminating her form. Dark hair spills around her face, making her skin look even paler than it already is. A trench coat covers her body, the belt cinched tight at the waist and accentuating her petite curves. Even from this distance, there's something tragic and forlorn about her, a sadness that seems to penetrate the very air that surrounds her.

When I close my eyes, I can still picture the look on her face in the park, that spark of desire, a longing for something she herself could not identify. So close. I was so close to doing something stupid. She's infecting me like a disease, an addiction for which there is no cure. That look told me she wants to be my dirty little obsession. And here I am. She has her wish.

It's late, and she's out here, walking alone in the dark. I'd be worried about someone attacking her, but I know the only thing out here she should truly fear is me. Waiting until she's slipped from sight, I get out of the car and lock it.

I remain on the opposite side of the road and walk slowly. She ducks through a small gate and up to the front door of one of the replica semi-detached houses that line the street. She fumbles with her keys, dropping them before picking them up. I remain across the street in the shadow of one of her neighbour's bushes. A guy walks along the pavement and pauses at the gate. He's wearing black jeans, a leather jacket and has a gait that screams of youth and arrogance.

"Lila." The street is utterly silent, and his voice carries through the night easily.

She freezes and whirls around. I can't see her face, but her body language is tense. He pushes through the gate and approaches her.

"Nate, now isn't a good time."

"It's never a good time. I'm not just letting you go, Lila."

"I can't talk to you right now." She shakes her head and goes to put her key in the door, but her hands are now trembling.

He grabs her shoulder, spinning her around and shoving her up against the door. I take a step forward out of the shadows, my fist already clenched and ready to break his jaw simply for touching her. But then I force myself to step back, disappointed at my momentary lack of self-control.

She speaks quietly to the guy before his fingers brush over her cheek. Then he leans in and kisses her, and something akin to rage twists in my gut. He isn't worthy of sweet Delilah.

After a moment she pushes him away and slips inside the house, slamming the door shut in his face. So the little lamb has a boyfriend. He takes his phone out and places it to his ear as he walks down the road.

"Yeah, it's me. I've got her under control. She won't talk." A pause. "It won't come to that. And you'll just draw more attention to the business," he hisses, his voice trailing off the farther away he gets.

The more I hear, the more that curiosity eats away at me. I debate following him when I see an upstairs light turn on in the house. Delilah moves around the room before releasing the button on her jeans and pushing them down her legs. I can see the top of her thong and about an inch of her arse, but it's enough. My dick twitches in my jeans and my fingers flinch as though they could trace the shape of her. Then she reaches for her tank and drags it over her head, exposing a white lace bra that matches her thong. Innocent and creamy and perfect. My cock hardens even more, and I step back, gripping the garden wall behind me to keep myself rooted.

Just as quickly as she stripped, she shoves a baggy t-shirt over her head. What the fuck am I doing? Pushing off the wall, I force myself to stride away from her house when truthfully, all I want to do is go back there and knock on the door. I want to desecrate her body in every way because I can't remember the last time I saw something so beautiful, so utterly pure, yet so devastatingly tainted.

But I can't. She's not ready. There will come a time when my little sinner tells me all — when she purges her soul to me like a sacrificial offering. And when she does, she's fair game.

———

I swear I can sense it, the second she walks in. Without even seeing Delilah, I know she's here in the church. I can't explain it, but she's like a storm. There's a tell-tale static in the air whenever she's near.

. . .

Once again, I linger in the doorway that separates the church from the offices at the back. She sits on the front pew. Her hands braced on her thighs, and her head dropped forward. She looks as though she has the weight of the world on her shoulders and it's slowly crushing her. Good. I want her broken and crumbling. I want her crawling on her knees for me, begging for salvation only I can give.

It's been five days since I last spoke to her. One since I saw her. But I knew she'd come. Her demons demand it of her. I see them dancing in her eyes, but they calm when I'm near because they recognise their own.

Stepping into the church, I approach her, but she never looks up, not even when I take a seat next to her. I wonder if she knows the inevitability of it all, or whether she still believes she can fight it. I know I should battle this irrational lure I have to her, but some things are fated, ordained. I don't believe that anything other than the Lord himself could have placed her in my path because she could be perfect.

I say the words that have been burning me for the last six days.

"You didn't come to confession." Not one day this week.

.   .   .

On a heavy sigh, she lifts her head and stares at the Virgin. "It doesn't help," she says, the hush of her voice carrying around the empty church.

"Then why come?"

She turns to face me, and I can almost see the cracks in her, she's so fractured. "Because you help," she breathes.

"God places people in your path for a reason." I want her to believe that.

She closes her eyes. "Just for today, don't be a priest. Please. I came to see a friend."

"Oh?"

Her eyes flash open. "I was hoping he might want a sushi repeat."

There's a look in her eye, a sorrow so deeply ingrained it is as though it's branded on her soul, and that...that calls to me like a flame calls to a moth. Ah, sweet, tainted Delilah. She thinks I can save her, but little does she know that she asks the devil for salvation.

· · ·

"I was about to head home. Come on." I stand and offer her my hand. As always, when she slides her palm over mine, there's that inherent sense of warmth like coming home after you've been away for a long time.

As we leave the church and walk down the street, she slips her hand into the crook of my arm, holding on like she's walking on sheet ice, and I'm the only thing keeping her upright. I frown down at her just as the wind catches a strand of her hair, blowing it across her face. What is it about her? Why do I pity her? Why do I want to ruin her and save her at the same time?

"Are you going to tell me what's wrong?" I ask. I shouldn't care, but I do. God, I do. I want all those sins to fall from her pretty lips like raindrops in a storm

Her step falters and then she stops until we're standing still in the middle of the street with people parting around us. "Do you ever spend so long running from your demons that you just can't see a way out anymore?"

"No." I don't run from my demons. I embrace them.

"Of course not. You don't have demons. You're a priest." She drops her head in shame and her shoulders sag. Reaching out, I press my finger beneath her chin, bringing her gaze to mine.

. . .

"We all have demons, Delilah." Ah, yes, there they are, dancing around in those pretty, sad eyes of hers. *Just let them play, little lamb.*

"Somehow I don't believe that *you* do." We stand in silence, people milling past us, and yet it's as though we're the only two people in the world right now.

"Come on. It's cold out here." I move to grab her arm, but instead, catch her hand. Her fingers wind through mine, and she doesn't let go. Instead, she clings on for dear life. And I let her.

We walk like that to my Thames-side apartment. Once inside, I close the door and take her coat, sliding it over her shoulders. She bends over, unzipping her knee-length boots and forcing the material of her black long-sleeved dress to ride up her milky thighs. I stand, rooted, my eyes trained on the exact spot where the material ends and her skin starts. Fuck. Clenching my fists, I stop myself from reaching out and touching her. Instead, I force myself to move past her, down the hall and into the kitchen. Taking items out of the fridge, I start putting them on the counter and placing pans on the cooker. I can feel her eyes burning a hole in my back, but I need a minute to pull myself together. I want to be Delilah's weakness, but it's not without cost because she's surely becoming mine.

. . .

When I do finally look at her, it doesn't help. She's taken off her boots, but in their place are knee-high woolly socks. They should look ridiculous, or at the least make her look childish. They do neither.

"Would you like a drink?" I ask, lifting my eyes to her face.

She nervously tucks her hair behind her ear. "Do you have wine?"

I nod and go to the fridge, taking out the bottle of white. I don't hear her approach, but her arm slides beneath mine as I finish pouring, her chest pressing to my back for a fleeting second before she snags the glass and moves away. I watch her retreat with a small smile on her face as she lifts it to her lips. *Careful, little lamb. You might get bitten.*

By the time I've cooked the steaks and placed them down on the dining room table, I'm tense, on edge and questioning why the hell I'm even bothering to keep myself in check. Fuck dinner. I should just throw her over the breakfast island and sink into her. She wants it. It's written all over her innocent face. The only thing stopping it is me. And why? Because I don't want to shatter the illusion. I need her to believe the lie. To trust me, to confess. She must confess.

I watch as she cuts a piece of steak and places it in her mouth, allowing the fork to slide past her lips.

.   .   .

"I wasn't sure you would come back," I say. "I thought I'd scared you off."

"I was embarrassed." Her fork clinks against her plate, and I'm not sure if she's about to get up and walk out. Instead, she drags both hands through her hair, her eyes falling closed. A long breath slips from her lips. "Judas, you've been a good friend to me. And I really need a friend right now." Those swirling grey irises collide with mine. "So, I'm sorry if I was inappropriate on Sunday. I promise it won't happen again." A friend? My eyes drop to her lips, her chest, then her tiny waist. There's nothing friendly about this.

"You weren't inappropriate," I say, trying not to recall the image of Delilah sucking ice cream off her finger. "And that's why you didn't come to confession?" She nods. God, she's so innocent, so perfectly pure in her unseen depravity.

She offers me a tight smile and picks up her fork again. She begins to ask me questions, about anything and everything, as though she's hungry for every fragmented detail about me.

"So, let me get this right. You're called Judas, and your brother is called Saint." I nod, and she shakes her head.

.   .   .

"When Ma had Saint she said that our father was a heathen and the kid needed all the help he could get." I laugh because it's so true.

"And is your dad a heathen?" Her lips twist in amusement.

"You could say that."

"And yet, you're a priest... What does your brother do?"

I'm treading carefully, telling the truth while omitting everything. "He owns a couple of nightclubs."

"Do you get on?"

I bite back a laugh. "Saint is...a little strange." She tilts her head to the side, delicately twirling the stem of the wine glass in her hand. "He thinks differently to the rest of us." She nods, seemingly satisfied with my half-truths and bullshit. "And you, Delilah, seem like an only child to me."

"What makes you say that?"

Because you always seem so inherently alone. "Just a feeling."

. . .

She swallows heavily, placing her glass to her lips. "You're good," she murmurs, before taking a sip. She's on her second glass, and I'm tempted to ply her with a third. Just to see what happens when sweet Delilah gets drunk.

Without a word, she gets up and takes both plates to the kitchen, running them under the tap. I watch her wash the plates, and I imagine her doing this; eating dinner, washing dishes, in another man's house. I get a small glimpse of the life she could lead one day if I were to leave her be. If I were to let her live in her continued denial. She could remain sweet Delilah, her sins buried and her darkness chained. She could marry a nice man and live a good life, a lie. The thought annoys me.

Moving behind her, I reach out, my fingers brushing over her hip. She stills before slowly turning to face me. There are barely a couple of inches of space between us, and she's caged against the sink.

Her eyes meet mine; the palette of greys swirling like a tornado. "Judas," she breathes, her hand landing on my chest, right over my heart. Her lips part and a trembling breath slips past them as her cheeks stain a pretty rose pink. "What are you doing?" she whispers.

"I don't know." Truthfully, for once, I don't. I just...need to touch her. I need to feel the warmth of her skin, smell the sweet vanilla scent that clings to her hair.

. . .

"You do." She reaches up, dragging her nails over the stubble on my jaw.

We stand on a precipice because once this starts, there's no stopping it. I'm too invested to turn from this path. "You should tell me to stop, Delilah," I warn. One last chance.

Her hand moves, and she drags her thumb over my bottom lip in a caress. "No," she whispers.

My eyes flash open, and I allow her to see the warning in them, to see a glimpse of the man I truly am. She doesn't flinch, so I fist a handful of her hair and slam my lips over hers. God, she's everything I thought she would be: sweetness and warmth, and pure compliance. She stills for a moment before softening in my hold. I take everything that I can from sweet Delilah. Her body bows and contorts to my will, her lips parting on desperate breaths and unwittingly allowing me entrance. She tastes like vanilla, and sugar, and the crispness of white wine. My hold on her hair tightens, and my teeth scrape her bottom lip until the tiniest hint of coppery blood explodes over my tongue. It's violent and unrestrained, but I have no sweet nothings to give her, only ruination. And through all this, her hands remain gentle, cupping my face, stroking over my chest. We're darkness and light, hard against soft, the tainted against perfection. We're a storm, and I want to throw my head back and bask in the deep rumble of thunder, the ironic thrill of being powerless and turning yourself over to something greater.

When I pull away, she's gasping for breath, and her lips are swollen and flushed a deep pink. She looks scandalised and violated, and it's making my dick hard. Her fingers press to her lips, and when she pulls them away, blood tinges the tips.

"Sorry," I say, but I'm not.

She trails her fingers over my lips. "Don't apologise." I nip at her fingertip, and she drops her hand. I'm this close to throwing her over that breakfast bar and shoving that dress up. I just want her. I don't know why, and I don't know how it's come to this, but I'm losing control. It's not time yet. I'm a man who always gets what he wants, but I know this little lamb isn't yet prepared to be devoured by the big bad wolf.

"You should go, Delilah," I grate out, forcing myself to step away from her.

Her eyes go wide before I watch the hurt rise in them.

She nods. "Yeah, I'll... Yeah."

.   .   .

She slips past me and into the hallway. I grip the kitchen counter until I hear the front door close, and then in a rare loss of control, I turn and launch the whiskey glass across the room.

12

DELILAH

I'm so stupid. What was I thinking? How did I get that so wrong?

Judas doesn't want me. Or maybe he does? He kissed me like he does. He kissed me like he wanted to crawl inside of me and live there. As though he would devour me and enjoy every second of it. He felt like a man on the edge, possessed, and god how I wanted that demon inside him to split in two and invade every inch of me.

But now I don't know what to do. Lines have blurred, and I'm terrified because I need him. He's the one person I can't lose, and though the pull I feel towards him goes far deeper than just friendship, I'll take what I can get. I'm scared he might not want to see me again. After all, he's a priest. He's taken a vow. I don't want to be a point of anguish, an unwanted temptation.

And of course, permeating all this is an incessant, nauseating feeling in the pit of my stomach. It's like the dial on my guilt has been cranked up to max because I kissed a guy. I should be thinking about a hundred other things right now except the one thing I am: Judas's lips. I'm guilty for not feeling guilty. Judas makes it a little easier to breathe, and when I'm with him, I forget about everything else. But the simple fact is that Izzy isn't out there kissing boys or inappropriately crushing on priests.

Round and round it goes. A never-ending cycle of self-persecution.

I leave my final lecture of the day and go to the library to pick up a book that I need for a research paper. I reach for the door, tugging it open, but it's slammed closed in front of me. Turning my head to the side, I come face to face with Nate.

I glance around nervously. "What are you doing here?" I hiss.

He grabs my wrist and pulls me back down the steps and to the side of the building. "You're back to ignoring my calls?" There's a feral glint in his eyes, and his actions are jittery.

"I've been busy," I say cautiously.

He shakes his head, his nostrils flaring with the action. "Summer said you were gone all day Sunday. She said you're out every night and come home late."

I yank my wrist away from him. "Fuck you, Nate. You're listening to Summer now?"

In the blink of an eye, his hand is at my throat, and he shoves me back against the wall. Rough brick scratches over the exposed skin of my arms, and I push against his chest, my heart beating like a hummingbirds wings. "Whatever the fuck is going on with you, sort it out."

"I don't think we should see each other anymore," I say in a rush.

He barks a laugh. "Oh, no, Lila. You're mine. We're done when I say we are done." He releases my throat and takes a step back. "I told you I love you, and I meant it. You sort yourself out, and everything can go back to how it was." He presses his lips to mine, but I twist my head to the side.

Without another word, he turns on his heel and stalks away. I stand there, my mouth opening and closing because words have completely escaped me. Nate's gone crazy. I slide down the wall, feeling my top catch and the threads pull, but I don't care. My whole life feels like a ticking time bomb just waiting to implode, and when it does, I'm going to be left with nothing, not even myself.

Shoving to my feet, I go into the library and find the book I need before leaving campus. I take the bus straight to the church and linger in front of the doors, not really wanting to go in but needing to, so badly. This is all I seem to have anymore. The only sanctuary from my festering soul.

I push open the door on a heavy groan of the hinges. The incense instantly calms my nerves, and I exhale, letting go of the tension that has turned my shoulders to stone.

The confessional booth sits to the side of the church as always, but today it feels so much more ominous than normal. I make my way to it, my heels clicking over the rugged stone floor. As soon as I step inside and pull the curtain, I feel like I can't breathe.

"Welcome," he says, and I hold my breath, saying nothing as I cross myself. There's a long beat of silence.

"Forgive me, father, for I have sinned," I whisper. "It's been over a week since my last confession." More silence. Then the rough timber of his voice.

"Tell me your sins, Delilah," Judas says, sounding more like the devil than the priest I know he is.

"I..." My voice trails off, and my cheeks flush.

"You can tell me anything," he lures again. The problem

is that he is now my sin, but I don't know that I can confess that.

"I've been having impure thoughts." I hesitate, and he remains silent. "But, these thoughts distract me from my more grievous sin. I know it's not right, but I don't know what to do."

"What kind of impure thoughts?"

"Carnal thoughts," I breathe.

"Then you should confess them, purge your soul." His voice has that sensual edge to it that I don't think he's even aware of.

"I'm having them about a man that I shouldn't."

"Go on."

"He's been a good friend to me, his intentions pure. I feel that I've put him in an uncomfortable position."

There's another pregnant pause, and the air in the confessional becomes thick and cloying. My heart thumps erratically against my chest, and my breaths come in short, sharp pants.

"Why do you think that?"

"Because he is bound by a vow that I know he would not wish to break. I think…I think that I am simply an unwanted temptation to him." I wish I could see his face.

"How do you know that his intentions are pure?"

"He's a good man."

"Is he?" he asks, the word layered in questions and implications.

"Is he?" I ask the question back at him. And now I'm starting to wonder. The tension lingers heavily in the space between us. Unspoken words. Untold promises. Whispered possibilities, and the absolute knowledge that this is undoubtedly a sin. Here of all places.

And the question remains unanswered. *Is he?*

13

JUDAS

MY DICK IS PRESSED against my fly, and my spine is ramrod straight. I force my hands to remain on my thighs, even as my fingers clench into fists. This girl...

Of course, I could simply forgive her for her sin and send her on her way, but I won't. I want her to break for me, to spill her dirty little secrets, to confess that which plagues her so vigilantly. I want to grasp this tiny loose thread and tug until she unravels at my feet and gives me the darkest parts of herself. I will corrupt her, one beautiful sin at a time.

"Do you think of him when you're alone at night?" I murmur into the darkness of the confessional, releasing the words into the world like a bullet, non-returnable and with unpredictable consequences.

"Yes," she whispers, that one word so perfect on her lips.

"And what if he thinks of you too?"

"Does he?" I smile as she teeters on that cliff edge, just waiting for me to push her because she wants to fall. I can feel it. She craves the abyss, the absolute depravity of bathing in her sins without apology. She wants the wrongness of it all. And don't we all? The Bible would tell you that the Devil waits to tempt us into sin, but the truth is that by nature, we are all sinners. We can't help ourselves. We're addicted to our own mortal demise. And sweet little Delilah has no idea that I'm the biggest sinner of them all. She's barely keeping her head above the surface of those dark waters, and I'm the monster that lurks in the deep, waiting to grab her ankle and pull her under.

"This isn't my confession. Delilah."

"What if it was?"

"You want me to confess to you?" Well, now, this just became interesting.

"Yes. You tell me yours, and I'll tell you mine. Do you think of me?" My muscles are bunched so tight it's painful, and I want to spill my deepest darkest thoughts. Just for her.

"Constantly." One word that signals the start of our little game. "And now I know what you taste like. It's intoxicating. I imagine what you would look like beneath me, moaning my name." I hear her hitched breath on the other side of the divider. *Yes, that's it, Delilah.* "How beautiful I know your body will be beneath those little dresses."

"Judas…"

"I imagine how you would feel wrapped around me."

There's another gasp from the other side of the partition and my cock twitches, becoming painful.

"I dreamt that you fucked me last night," she admits on a rasped whisper. I bite back a groan at her perfect confession.

"What did I do to you?" I ask through gritted teeth, shoving my fly down and releasing myself.

"You bent me over the altar…"

"Fuck!" I hiss, grabbing my dick, stroking over the length of it. Such a dirty, filthy little sinner she is.

"Then you grabbed my hair, just like you did when you

kissed me." Her words are broken by a soft moan that has every muscle in my body coiling tight.

"I want to ruin you, Delilah."

"God, yes." Her hand presses up against the partition, fingers curling into the mesh as though she could reach through it.

Shit. I press my free hand to hers, our skin meeting through the intricate mesh . Her touch, that breathy little hitch in her voice, the image her words have placed in my mind...it all culminates to a point until everything tightens and then explodes outward in release. Warm liquid seeps over my hand, and I grit my teeth against the low groan that tries to work up my throat. I just came all over my own hand...in the confessional. It's perverse even by my standards.

Our palms remain pressed to the divider for long moments before I finally allow mine to slip away. I have no way of cleaning up, so I simply zip my trousers and push to my feet.

"Goodbye, Delilah," I say, unable to keep the smirk off my face.

"Goodbye, father." That shouldn't be hot, but it is. The girl is the devil in disguise, and oh, how I want her.

14

DELILAH

Stepping outside the church, the fresh air washes over my heated cheeks. Rounding the side of the building, I slip into the shadows of the graveyard. I don't spot the figure in front of me until I've collided with a hard chest.

"Sorry," I mumble, looking up. It takes a few seconds for me to process Nate's deep chocolate gaze focused on me. "Nate? What are you doing here?"

"I could ask you the same."

I frown, peering around him and spotting his car parked on the side of the road just behind us. "How did you know I was here?"

"I followed you."

"You…" My eyes go wide, and my hands tremble slightly, so I shove them in my pockets. "I took the bus here," I say, more to myself than him. He says nothing, leaving me to put the pieces together. He followed the bus. And then my stomach drops like a lead balloon. Is it possible that he heard my confession?

I take in his clenched fists, the rigid set of his shoulders, and his lips pressed tightly together. Reaching out, he snatches my arm and drags me to the car. I'm so startled that I don't react until I'm in the car and he's pulling away. His fingers wrap around the steering wheel so tightly that his knuckles turn white. He revs the engine, gunning it through the busy London traffic. Tyres screech as he tears around a corner, never letting up.

"Nate, you're scaring me," I say.

He laughs. "Oh, sweetheart, you have no idea."

We stop outside his apartment complex. I've only been here a couple of times, but right now I'd rather be anywhere else. I try the door handle, but it won't give. He flashes me a wicked smirk before getting out and rounding the front. I'm yanked from the car so hard that he twists my wrist, and I cry out.

"Nate!"

"Shut the fuck up," he growls, pulling me towards the front of the building. My heart is racing so hard and fast that I'm practically choking on it. I fight him as he shoves me in the elevator, but it's pointless. If I scream will anyone help me? Or will it just make him mad? I don't have time to think about it though. We're at his apartment door, and in the next instant we're inside, and I'm on my own.

Slowly, I back away from him and he stalks me.

"You thought you could go behind my back?" he snarls, his face contorted in rage. I say nothing, terrified to set him off. "With that fucking priest?" He tilts his head to the side. "You think I don't know what goes on at that church? You trying to cut me out, hey, Lila? Thought you'd move up in the world? Was this whole 'I feel so guilty thing' all just bullshit so you could fuck me over?" He sounds like a rambling madman. My silence just seems to make him angrier, and he charges at me, his hand slamming around my throat as he shoves me backwards onto the coffee table. My legs buckle, and he forces my spine to contort over the wood. Terror consumes every inch of my brain, and I gasp for breath, the sound coming out as a choked sob. "Trying to break up with me... trying to cut me out." His fingers tighten around my throat and tears stream down my temples. Black spots dot my vision, and I know he's going to kill me. It's nothing less than I deserve, right? "You're mine!" he roars, releasing me. I suck in a huge breath, just as something collides with the side of my face so hard that for a moment I can't see. Pain explodes across my cheek, my head swims, and then everything goes black.

When I come to, Nate is a few feet away, pacing across the room. "Fuck!" he shouts, dragging both hands through his hair. My head is spinning, my ears ringing so loudly that all I can hear is my own breaths rasping in time with the throbbing beat. The entire left side of my face feels like it's on fire and the metallic taste of copper fills my mouth. *He's going to kill me. He's going to kill me.* The thought repeats like an alarm and survival kicks in. Rolling over, I fall to the carpet on my hands and knees. I watch as heavy drops of blood fall to the ground in front of me. *Drip, drip, drip.* Leaving a trail of gruesome breadcrumbs as I crawl across the room to the window. Dragging myself to my feet, I wrap my fingers around the vase on the windowsill and lift it, bringing it down hard. The glass shatters, and I wince when it slices through my hand.

"What the fuck..."

I whirl around, brandishing a huge shard of shattered glass. "Stay the fuck away from me," I cry, tears blinding me. My hand shakes and my legs feel numb and unsteady as I slowly shuffle towards the other side of the room. He mirrors me, stalks me. I back towards the front door and push the handle down. I just have to get to the other side. "Follow me, and I'll scream," I choke out.

His eyes narrow, and I know with that one look that he won't let this go. The door closes between us, and I run, as fast as my weakened legs will carry me. I run all the way to the only person I want to see right now. By the time I reach the church, I can't breathe. Tears pour uncontrollably down my face, and my entire body trembles as a bone-deep cold settles over me. I stagger up the steps and hope to God that Judas is here.

"Judas." My voice cracks.

The building welcomes me like the warm embrace of a doting mother. A safe haven, but even so, I glance over my shoulder as I make my way down the aisle, sure that Nate must have followed me. I trip, falling to my knees right in front of the Virgin. Blood drips from my face, hitting the worn stone beneath me, and I can't help but think that it looks like some kind of twisted sacrificial offering.

"Delilah?" Closing my eyes, I smile. *Judas*. His voice feels like the Lord himself whispering in my ear, soothing me. "Delilah?" He drops to a crouch in front of me, and I see his hand land among the drops of blood. I lift my head, and his eyes take in my face, slowly widening in horror. "Fuck." He goes to touch me but hesitates, then his gaze drops to my hand. He carefully wraps his fingers around the piece of bloodied glass that I hadn't even realised I was still clutching. "Just...let go." I do, wincing as my fingers unfurl, opening up the deep slices across my palm. More blood hits the stone, and I wonder if the Virgin will consider it enough to forgive me of my sins now. "Who did this to you?" I open my mouth to speak but the pain radiates through my jaw, and my lip splits farther, making blood pool in my mouth. "You need to go to a hospital."

I shake my head and utter the word, no. If I go to a hospital like this, the police will be involved. They'll ask questions. Nate might think I've turned him in. He'll come after me. I shiver at the thought.

Wordlessly, he scoops me up, cradling me against his chest. Pain throbs through my temples, my face, my back, my hand...but he grounds me. He makes it all a little less horrifying.

It's not until he places me on a desk in some kind of office that the true gravity of what just happened sets in. My muscles lock down until my entire body is trembling, and then I just cry, fat ugly tears permeated by the strangled sobs tearing from my throat. Judas simply pulls me against his chest and holds me. My fingers knot in his shirt, clinging onto him as though he were a safety net suspended over a death-defying drop. I need him. I always need him, and I know that's wrong of me. When the tears slow and the sobs quiet, he disappears and comes back first with an ice pack, then with a first aid kit, a bowl of water and a cloth. He methodically washes my hand, his brows furrowing as he squints, inspecting my palm closely for any stray pieces of glass. Then he places little butterfly stitches along the cut and bandages it. I sit with the ice pressed to my face, watching his deliberate, yet gentle movements.

When he's done, his eyes meet mine. Gone is the panic, and now I can see something else lurking in those clear blue depths: rage. On a ragged sigh, he lifts his hand and carefully lowers the ice pack. "I need to know who did this to you, Delilah." I close my eyes, inhaling a sharp breath. His fingers gently trail over the uninjured side of my face, and I lean into his warmth. "I don't care what trouble you're in. Just let me help you."

"You can't help me," I whisper, fresh tears now breaking free.

He leans forward, touching his forehead to mine. "Give me a name. That's it. No police, I promise." There's something in his voice, a barely concealed threat, the promise of retribution, and I want it. I want Nate to hurt. I want him to feel powerless. I just don't want to stain Judas's soul.

"You can't go after him."

He lifts his face, pressing his lips to my forehead in a feather-light kiss. "Just a name, little lamb."

I hesitate, but I can't keep it from him. How can I? I would give Judas anything he asked of me. "Nate," I breathe. "My...ex-boyfriend. He...he knows, about you." Judas stills. "About us."

"Thank you."

He leaves the room, and when he comes back, it's with fresh water and a clean cloth. He stands between my legs and places a gentle finger to my chin, twisting my face to the side.

"This'll sting," he says before placing the cloth to my bloodied lip. It does sting, but I embrace the pain as I stare at him. My body hurts, my heart is wounded, and my soul is broken, but in his eyes, I feel lost and found all at once.

"Do you feel sick or dizzy?"

"A little."

He lifts my hand that's clutching the dripping ice pack and presses it to my face. "Can you walk?" I nod, and he moves away, taking his coat from the back of the door. "Put this on. You're freezing." I don't realise just how cold I am until he says it. I get up and slide my arms into the heavy material, pulling the over-sized coat tight around me. It smells of him: citrus and incense.

Placing an arm around my shoulders, he pulls me into

his side and leads me straight through the church. I barely look up from the shadow of his body until we're at his apartment building. Wordlessly he opens the door and guides me inside.

"You should stay here a while. I can take you home later." My breaths shorten at the thought of going home. Nate knows where I live. What if he turns up? Placing my hand to my chest, I try and swallow down the debilitating fear. "Hey. Hey." Judas cups my face. "He won't touch you, I promise." His words are calm, softly spoken, but his expression is the polar opposite. There's something feral and uncontrolled raging behind his eyes, and I'm both scared of it and thrilled by it because I know that Judas would never hurt me. I know it in the depths of my soul because he's a good man. "You can stay here as long as you want."

I press my forehead against his chest, and his arms come around me, his palms smoothing over my back. "Thank you," I whisper, fighting back yet more tears. As if I wasn't a mess before, now I'm a simpering wreck.

As the adrenaline that fired through my veins lessens, the more the pain all starts to kick in. Judas takes something out of a drawer and pours me a glass of water before handing me several pills. "Take those. They'll help." I do as he says without question and a small smile touches his lips. "You should lie down."

Again, like the obedient little lamb he calls me, I follow him down a hallway to a bedroom. The citrus of his cologne hangs heavy in the air, and I know that this is his room. I stand there awkwardly for a moment, unsure what to do.

He smirks before turning to a chest of drawers and taking out a t-shirt. "You can wear this."

"Thanks."

I try to fumble with the small buttons on my shirtdress,

but with one bandaged hand, the fiddly buttons are near impossible. Eventually, he pushes me away and takes over. I lift my eyes from the buttons to his face and find his gaze firmly locked on mine. And that's where it stays, even as the material separates, and I feel the rush of cool air over my stomach. He turns me away from him, and I shrug the dress over my shoulders, allowing it to pool at my feet. There's the audible sound of a sharp breath, and I shiver, before sliding his soft t-shirt over my head. Pulling back the covers, I climb into his bed, my head already foggy and my eyelids heavy.

Judas disappears from the room and comes back a few moments later wearing only a pair of tracksuit bottoms. My eyes suddenly have no problem staying wide open, and I'd be surprised if my jaw isn't gaping, though I can't feel it through the incessant throbbing.

I'm not sure a man has ever been more perfect. Just miles of tanned skin over taut, honed muscles. An enormous tattoo of an angel sits on his chest, the wings arching high and spreading right up to his shoulders. When I catch a glimpse of his back, I see a plain black cross that spans his shoulders and stops about half way down his spine. It's not pretty or ornate, just simple, thick, black lines. Everything about him is just...art. If he notices me looking, he doesn't say anything. Instead, he slides into the bed next to me and gently pulls me close. My good cheek lands on his chest and the heat of his skin sears me like a brand because at this point, I honestly think Judas is imprinting himself on me: mind, body and soul.

I've kissed him. I think about him every hour of every day, and now he's here, holding me when I need it most. Fingers stroke through my hair and his lips press to my scalp, caressing, caring, piecing me back together one touch at a time. I had no idea how badly I needed this, needed him.

The fog in my head swims thick and fast, and the heavy tempo of Judas's heartbeat is like the ticking of a hypnotist's clock, lulling me, deeper, deeper...until sleep overcomes me.

15

JUDAS

I LAY THERE FOR A WHILE, listening to Delilah's soft breaths. Her chest rises and falls gently, her fingers twitching against my stomach every so often. She feels so small tucked into me like this, so trusting. I close my eyes, and all I see is her — on her hands and knees on the church floor, blood everywhere. Glancing down, I can still make out the bruising that's blossoming over her cheek, her throat.

He touched her. He hurt her. And the rage that's burning in me is threatening to scorch me from the inside out. After an hour of making sure her breaths remain even, I slip away from her. She doesn't stir. One of the pills I gave her was a sedative because I need her to sleep. I need her to be completely unaware that I ever left.

I pull the door closed with a muted click and go to the living room. Taking out my laptop, I pull up Facebook and type her name in. Delilah Thomas. She pops up, and I quickly find a picture of her and the guy I saw the night I followed her. He has no Facebook account, but a picture is enough.

Taking out my phone, I send a text.

Me: Hey. I need you to find everything you can on this guy. First name is Nate. I'm sending you money now.

I attach the picture and then do as I said, logging into the app and sending across three grand. The finder's fee.

Jase: Give me ten minutes.

Ten minutes later and an email pings up. There's an image of a drivers license, an arrest record of petty drug charges, and a home address. Nathaniel Hewitt. Twenty-four years old. He's also sent me a mobile phone number and a link. Clicking on it, it's a map, with a blinking green dot on it. He's in Soho.

My phone pings again.

Jase: *Heads up. Pretty sure this guy works for the Moretti's.*

Even more reason for me to kill him. I have to wonder if Delilah knows.

Slipping back into the bedroom, I silently get changed into a pair of jeans and a black t-shirt. Delilah rolls over, a soft sigh falling from her lips. She looks so small in my bed, but so right. My heart thumps heavily, and a strange feeling settles into my chest. I've never even bothered with women past a few nights of pleasure, never understood the concept of love. But as I look at her, so beautiful, so broken, I realise love pales in comparison to this...obsession. There's very little I wouldn't do to have her.

Moving closer, I gently stroke a strand of deep brown hair away from her face. Even in sleep, she leans into my touch, and I smile, pressing my lips to her forehead.

"I'll make it right, sweet Delilah," I whisper.

I grip the steering wheel, my teeth grinding over each other as I watch the apartment building. It's nearly midnight, and the street is quiet. My phone is hooked into the car, and the screen on the dash shows a map of the surrounding area. I watch as that blinking green dot moves, fast enough to be a car. Closer, closer, until I finally see a black BMW come screeching around the corner at the top of the road. The engine is obnoxiously loud, breaking through the peacefulness of the street. It parks on double yellow lines, and someone gets out, walking up to the front of the building. I'm out of the car and crossing the road before he even reaches the door. Just as he slides his key in the lock, I step up behind him, palming the knife in my pocket and pressing it to the side of his throat. He stills, lifting his hands.

"Walk inside, go to your apartment."

He pushes the door open and steps inside slowly. "You're fucking with the wrong person."

I huff a laugh under my breath but say nothing. The kid has no idea what's coming, and honestly, I'm not sure I do either. This rage is riding me so hard that I know I can't trust myself to be rational or restrained, but I'm here because I don't care. I'm not planning to kill him because killing people is messy. There's clean up and alibis, blah, blah, blah. That said, if he happens to die, I'll deal with it.

He moves up a flight of stairs and the entire time, I'm right there, breathing down his neck with cold steel pressed to his throat. Once inside his apartment, my temper gets the best of me, and I punch him. Blood explodes everywhere, and he cries out, clutching his badly-broken nose. I drag him by the scruff of his neck and dump him in the armchair in his living room. It's only when I turn the lamp on that I see the trail of rust red spots over his cream carpet. Fat drops of blood, leading to the window where pieces of glass dust the windowsill and carpet.

"That's her blood, isn't it?"

He looks up at me, his hand still clutched to his face and blood now streaming down his chin and pouring into his lap. "Who the fuck are you?"

I smile, my pulse calming and the heat in my veins dying down. The rage is still right there, but it becomes ice cold, calculating. I start picturing all the ways I could hurt him. All the ways I could make his last moments miserable.

"You might know me as Father Kavanagh, but my real name is Judas Kingsley." I say the words slowly, dramatically, drawing them out with a smile. There's a reason I go by the name Kavanagh, and it's because, in certain circles, the name Judas Kingsley comes with dire consequences. There was a time when I was every bit as feared as my brother. When I was young and foolish and wanted a reputation. His eyes narrow, and I can see the wheels turning, him piecing together everything he knows from threads of information.

His jaw sets and his chin lifts as he pushes to his feet. "You think Delilah will make you any money?" He lets out a laugh. "You're welcome to her."

I shove my hand in my pocket, sliding my fingers through the cool metal of my brass knuckles. My father's side of the family taught me business, but my mother's side of the family are Irish gypsies. They taught me that violence should always be brutal and memorable. Put a man down once properly, and he'll never rise again.

My arm swings back and smashes into his face. I smile at the satisfying crunching of his cheekbone, and the little demon that I try to keep leashed dances around his fire. My fist pulls back again and again, nailing him in the gut, the ribs, mainly body shots. And when he's lying on the floor gasping for short breaths through cracked ribs and straining lungs, I pause. My chest rises and falls heavily, and my knuckles are bleeding where the brass has bitten into my skin. I don't care. His blood and mine mix together, coating my fist and smearing up the length of my forearm.

That demon is riding me hard, screaming at me to just land one last punch to his throat. Collapse his trachea, and watch him suffocate to death right before my eyes. You see, Saint and I aren't so different. I'm just better at hiding it.

I walk away, pacing for a few minutes. Nate just lies there. Gasping through rattling lungs. His fingers grip the arm of the couch, and I notice the splits in his right knuckles. From hitting Delilah. Glancing across the room, I spot some kind of bronze statue on his mantelpiece, an award of sorts. Picking it up, I toss it up and down in my hand, testing the weight.

Then I grab his wrist, wrenching him forward on a cry and slamming his palm on the coffee table.

"What are you—"

My arm arcs high into the air, and I bring the statue down hard over his hand. I swear I can hear the bones crack, and I smile. He screams, and I slam a hand over his mouth.

"Shut the fuck up." Tears form and fall down his cheeks, meeting my fingers. When he finally quiets, I remove my hand, and he whimpers like a kicked dog. "Stay away from her, or I'll make this look like a trip to Disneyland," I growl.

"You're fucking her, aren't you?" His voice is pained. I say nothing, allowing the assumption to go unchecked. "Does she know who you are?" Each word is a strained whisper.

Dropping to a crouch, I grab a handful of his hair and

wrench his head back. "*You* know who I am. And I know exactly who you are, who you work for, your entire tiny network. Go near her again, and I will destroy you." I stand, sneering at him. "You should be grateful I'm showing you mercy." I remove the knuckles and slip them into my pocket. "After all, I am a man of God."

When I get back to my apartment, Delilah is still asleep. I get in the shower, and the water runs red with blood: mine and Nathaniel's. It swirls down the drain, taking the night's events with it. I clench and release my fists, trying to dissipate the rage that's still sitting on my chest like a lead weight. I wanted to kill him. I needed to hurt him, and that lack of control bothers me. She shouldn't have so much power over me. I had a plan. I was going to be patient, but now he's ruined it.

When I finally step out of the shower, the very first rays of dawn are starting to creep over the horizon, turning the night sky grey. I slip into bed beside Delilah, pulling her against me. She settles with her back to my chest, and I kiss the side of her neck, inhaling the lingering hint of vanilla that remains on her skin. I wrap my arm around her waist, and she slides her hand over mine, holding on.

My chest squeezes tight, and I close my eyes, feeling both peaceful and chaotic at the same time. And she's the source of both, the cause and the consequence. She riles my demon and then she soothes him, petting him like a harmless kitten.

I wake to the feel of something stroking over my chest. Blinking my eyes open, I glance down at Delilah with her cheek pressed to my chest and her fingers drawing circles on my other pec. If she notices the hundreds of raised lines set into the angel's feathers, she doesn't say.

Her gaze is fixed on the wall, eyes distant. The bruising

on her face is darker this morning, purples and blues mixing and tarnishing her smooth skin.

"Hey."

She tilts her head back and looks at me. "Hey."

Neither of us says anything else for long minutes, and I wish I didn't have to, but the previous night lingers there between us. I can see that she's hurting, and I can see that she's still scared. She goes to chew her bottom lip but winces. A fresh bead of blood wells in the split, and I brush it away with my finger.

"He won't come near you again, Delilah."

She closes her eyes, swallowing on a deep breath. "I'm sure he won't."

"No, he won't." I accentuate my words, as I place a finger beneath her chin, forcing her to meet my gaze. "I promise."

"What did you do?" she whispers.

Shifting, I force her to sit up so I can move. I swing my legs over the edge of the bed and drag a hand through my hair. "Don't worry about it."

"Judas, what did you do?" she repeats, her palm landing on the bare skin of my back. It's like she's attached to the mains and a bolt of static straightens my spine.

I stare at the wall, at the abstract piece of art that Saint gifted me when I first moved in here. He loves his art. "I'm not who you think I am." The secrets lay between us like a minefield, and it suddenly feels impregnable. I want to tell her everything, but she's not ready. He's forcing my hand. Delilah may be a broken, troubled sinner, but she's a normal girl with a normal life. But then I remember Nathaniel's comment. *You think she'll make you money?* Or perhaps sweet Delilah is far more tainted than even I've given her credit for.

Her hand smooths down the length of my back. "Did…"

She inhales a sharp breath. "Did Nate say anything?" There's a tremor in her voice.

Glancing over my shoulder, I meet her gaze. The look in her eyes, her teeth scraping over the corner of her lip. She's scared. I watch her for a moment, reading her, seeing her.

"He knows, doesn't he?"

"Knows what?"

"Your sin."

Her eyes close and she drops her chin to her chest. It's all the answer I need. He knows. He knows, and I don't!

Bracing my back to the headboard, I grip her waist and yank her into my lap. She gasps in surprise, her palms landing on my chest. My t-shirt rides up her thighs as she straddles me and my heart rate ticks up. Taking her face in both hands, I force her to look at me. Nowhere left to run, little lamb.

"It's time for you to confess, Delilah."

"I can't."

"Please." I've never begged for anything in my life, but I need it. I need her sin like I need air.

"You'll hate me, Judas. I hate me." She chokes on her words.

"I'll confess mine if you confess yours," I offer, and there it is, the culmination of what should have taken months, all out there. Both our sins, on the table, the ugly darkness revealed. I'll gladly show her mine if I get to see hers.

She drops her head forward, and as she blinks, a single tear clings to her lashes before falling to her cheek. "It's not...it's not the same."

"How do you know?"

"You're a priest, Judas. You're good. And my sin..."

"I'm not good, little lamb."

She offers me a small smile. "How could you possibly be

bad?" She reaches up, stroking feather-light fingers over my lips. "You couldn't."

"Little do you know, sweet Delilah," I lean in close, nipping her earlobe, "For even Satan disguises himself as an angel of light."

16

DELILAH

I SHIVER at his words as what feels like the trail of an icy finger drags down my spine. I want to confess to him, I do. I want to pour all of the ugly guilt out, just so that someone else knows, someone else can shoulder some of it, and I know Judas will. But I'm terrified that I'll lose him. That he'll be so horrified that he won't be able to look at me.

I take his right hand, tracing my fingers over the raw scabbed-over skin that rings each finger. It wasn't there last night, I'm sure of it.

"So you're Satan?" I ask on a whisper. He says nothing. Our eyes lock. "Then confess to me, Judas."

His thumbs stroke over my jaw gently. "You first."

"That's...fair." He looks at me expectantly. Waiting. Those deep blue eyes search my soul, reading me like a book. "I don't think I can confess to you if I see you."

The corner of his lip pulls into a smirk. "Really?" I nod, and he simply moves me from his lap, gets up and steps outside the room, closing the door behind him. "How about now?" he says from the other side of the door.

I smile. "Yeah, that's...better."

I go to the door and slide to the ground, wincing as I press my bruised back to the wall beside it.

"Please don't hate me when this is done," I whisper, more to the universe than him.

"Never."

On a deep breath, I cross myself and begin. "Forgive me, father, for I have sinned. It's been one day since my last confession."

"I will hear your confession, Delilah."

Oh god. I think I'm going to be sick. My heart beats harder and faster until it's physically jolting my body. The air feels thin, and my vision swims. "I killed my friend," I gasp. "And I can't forgive myself." I press a hand over my mouth, trying to quench the sobs that want to break free. I hadn't realised how much I needed to speak the words. To confess them just like that, but now they're out there. He knows, and I can no longer hide the ugly stain that's spreading over me like blood in water. My heart breaks a little because I know; I just know that he'll look at me differently. He says nothing, and I can feel his judgement even through the wood of the door. Closing my eyes, I pull my knees to my chest and press my forehead to them. He's going to kick me out and never speak to me again. My ears are ringing, permeated only by the choking sound coming from my throat. I don't hear him open the door, merely feel the warmth of his arms as he scoops me up and sits on the floor, clutching me to his chest. My tears soak into his shirt as his fingers stroke through my hair. Why is he being so nice? He's a priest. He should be damning me to hell and kicking me out of his apartment. He should want no part of my sordid sin, but he's here. And I cling to him like he's the only island in a storm-battered ocean.

"Shh, it's fine." His lips press into my hair, his hot breath stirring the strands.

"I didn't mean to. I was…I gave her boyfriend some pills. She overdosed."

"Gave?"

"I was just delivering them."

"For Nate?" I nod, and his chest rises and falls on a heavy sigh beneath my cheek.

"I was a fool. I wanted to date the bad boy and be rebellious." He stills for a moment and then resumes stroking my hair. I lift my face from his chest, needing to see his eyes. I expect him to look horrified or repulsed, but he looks… relieved? "I tried to go to the police, but Nate said that the people he worked for would kill me if I did. I know I deserve that, but I was scared. Do you hate me?" I ask.

His brows pinch together in a frown, and he cups my face. "Delilah, you've never been more beautiful." I frown, his reaction throwing me off. "People sin all the time. They ask for forgiveness they don't really want, and for what? So they may go to a better place when they die. They don't embrace their sins. They don't suffer for them." A soft smile shapes his lips. "But you have suffered, and why? Your guilt is debatable."

"I'm guilty. I killed my friend," I whisper. "Aren't you supposed to tell me that I need to repent in order for God to forgive me?"

"But it's not his forgiveness you need, is it?" He twisted smile crosses his lips. "I think you should hear my confession."

"Okay."

He gets up, lifting me with him effortlessly before he places me down on the edge of the bed. He then stands, moving away from me and propping his back to the wall. He's putting space between us.

"Forgive me, Delilah, for I have sinned," he says. "It's been thirteen years since my last confession."

Thirteen? I say nothing and push that information aside.

Our gazes collide, and for the first time since I've known him, I see something...bad. His eyes dance dangerously, and he folds his arms over his tattooed chest, making him look broader and even more muscular. He looks natural like this, and I realise that everything I've seen of him before has been so very unnatural — forced.

"I'm not who you believe I am, Delilah."

I still. "Then who are you?"

Teeth scrape over his bottom lip, and his chest rises and falls on a heavy breath. "I'm not a real priest. Not a true believer as they would say."

"Okay..."

"I became a priest because it served a purpose."

"What purpose?" I whisper, not sure if I want the answer. I can feel it, this impending doom just lingering in the air. Everything is about to change.

"It's complicated, but let's just say it's for business purposes."

"What kind of business are you in, Judas?"

We stare at each other, and of course, I know what he's going to say because I always, always fall for the bad boy. Every time.

"Cocaine." One word. Like the cracking of a whip split-ting the air. Only he split something else: us. I feel the rip tear across the expanse between us, threatening to send me hurtling into an abyss from which I cannot return. I'm a sinner. He's a sinner. *He's a bad man.* The words repeat over and over in my mind, but the accompanying panic that should come with them remains curiously absent.

"So you're like Nate?"

"No, Delilah. I'd be the equivalent to Nate's bosses, bosses boss."

"The top of the food chain." The words are an uttered breath as realisation truly sinks in. Judas is the person profiting from people like me, people like Isabelle. He's the huge cog making the entire machine turn. Isabelle was a victim of that machine. I was a naïve participant. I feel sick to my stomach, and a throbbing starts behind my temples.

He says nothing, simply stands there and waits. "I need to go home," I finally muster.

To his credit, Judas opens the door and walks out. When I gingerly follow him, he's standing by the front door, keys in hand. "I'll drive you. You shouldn't be walking long distances," he says. His face is a mask that I haven't seen before. Hard, implacable. This is the real man behind the dog collar, the drug lord. I don't know this man, and yet, when I look in his eyes and spot a trace of pain, I hurt. I wish I could take it away, but right now I can't.

I'm caught in a tailspin of guilt and loathing, unable to move on, and just when I think I've found someone who may finally help me, finally absolve me in some way; he's worse than me. *Satan disguised as an angel of light.* Truer words have never been spoken.

The car ride is tense and silent. When he pulls up outside of my house, he stares straight ahead through the windscreen. Looking at my home, a shiver of fear works up my spine. Nate knows where I live. He might come for me. If he knows who Judas really is, he might heed his warning, but I can't rely on Judas protection. I don't want to.

He hands me something, and I glance down at my

phone in his hand. "My number is in it. If you need anything, call me."

I nod and grab the door handle, pulling it. But I hesitate before I get out. "Thank you for helping me, Judas. You're a good man." And then I get out of the car, those words ringing in my mind because I actually believe them.

17

DELILAH

When I get in, I dump my handbag on the kitchen counter and go to the fridge. There's a note stuck to it.

Just a reminder that the rent is due on Friday.
Tiff x

Shit. I thump my forehead against the fridge door. I have enough money to pay this month, but what about next month? I dealt for Nate because it was a rush, but the by-product of that was money. I never had to worry about getting a job to pay rent. But now...it's been nearly two months.

Mum doesn't have any money, and I'd rather starve than ask my father. I need a job, now. God, my life is such a train wreck.

Grabbing the orange juice from the fridge, I pour a glass and take it to my room. I've refused to look in a mirror, but I force myself now. Standing in front of my wardrobe, I stare at my reflection. The left side of my face is a kaleidoscope of blues, pinks, and purples. My bottom lip has a split right down the centre with a thick scab over it, and bruises ring my neck. Lifting my dress, I see the welts on my lower back, and of course, my bandaged hand. Now my outside looks just as messy as what is inside.

Taking a seat on the edge of the bed, I allow my head to fall into my hands. I'm a criminal, a drug dealer, and a killer. I have no money, no job, my ex-boyfriend just beat me up, and the friendly neighbourhood priest, who I trusted to help me, is, in fact, a drug lord. Great.

I jump in the shower, and then I get to work on trying not to look like an abuse victim. Taking out my make up bag, I start to carefully apply thick layers of foundation over the bruising on my face. A swipe of mascara, a little blush, and I don't look half as washed out as I feel. I don't manage to cover the purple hue completely, but close enough. There's not a lot I can do about my lip, and I toss a silk scarf around my neck to cover the marks at my throat.

A navy shirtdress and some knee-high boots, and I'm good to go. I don't even bother to dry my hair before leaving the house.

I sit through four lectures, trying to pay attention, trying to take down notes, but I'm jittery. I keep looking over my shoulder — sure that Nate is about to jump out from some corner. Judas said Nate wouldn't touch me again, but how does he know? My thoughts trip over themselves at that. Did he kill him? Would he? He's a criminal. Of course he would.

At the end of my last lecture, I leave the hall and head for the library. I'm behind on a paper on Gandhi, and I need a particular book that can't be checked out. I'd buy it, but seeing as I can barely make rent... I find a table, get the books I need and work. I'm so distracted that I hardly notice it's grown dark outside. I turn on the desk lamp and glance around the library, realising that there's only me and one other guy in here. The elderly librarian is propped behind the desk, her head lolling to one side and her glasses sitting at a jaunty angle as she falls asleep.

The man is sitting on a chair in the corner. His head tilted down as he reads a book. He looks a little old to be in here, but then he could be a mature student or a lecturer. Closing up my book, I put all my things in my rucksack and stand up. My bruised body has seized up from sitting too long, and I wince, my steps short and awkward as I make my way to the door. When I shoulder the door open, my gaze happens to travel to the corner where that one man was sitting. He's gone.

I step outside and my heartbeat flitters in my chest. I'm alone. The steps of the library drop into a square courtyard surrounded by trees. The wind rustles through the leaves, sending shadows reaching and writhing through the dim orange glow cast by the streetlights. I find myself scanning the shadows, looking for threats everywhere. What if Nate's out here again? I've just reached the bottom of the steps when the library door bangs closed behind me. Glancing over my shoulder, I see the man with the book, his tall, thin frame towering at the top of the steps. Part of me thinks I should stay with him, in case Nate is out here, but he looks dodgy. He could work for Nate for all I know. Before I can think it through, I start striding across the courtyard, as fast as my stiff legs will carry me.

I'm too late for the last bus, so I'll have to walk home. I've gone a few streets when I tilt my head and hear quickened footsteps following maybe a few meters behind. When I look, I see the same straggly figure as before. He's following me. Or he's just walking this way, and it's a coincidence? *Says every girl who ever got raped, murdered, and dismembered.* Panic rises like a wave, hard and fast, drowning out rational thought.

Without thinking about it, I speed up and take out my phone, pressing Judas's name because who else am I going to call? I have no one. It rings and goes to voicemail. Fuck. My house is fifteen minutes away. The church is five. Breaking into a run, I head in that direction. Over my heavy breaths, I'm sure I can hear footsteps behind me. My heart slams against my ribs and adrenaline overrides any pain I might have been in a few minutes ago.

Staggering up the church steps, I still don't feel safe. Glancing around frantically, I spot the confessional box and run to it, diving behind the curtain and pulling it closed. My breathing is so loud I might as well be throwing a party in here, and I do my best to quiet it. I hear approaching foot-steps on the stone floor, and I back up in the tiny space, regretting my decision to come in here because there's no escape. The material of the curtain bunches and pulls where someone has grabbed it, and then it's torn back, sending my heart dropping through the floor.

"Delilah?" Judas frowns at me. I've never been so happy to see anyone.

"Judas," I breathe, grabbing him and yanking him inside. I tear the curtain shut and close my eyes for a second, leaning my head back against the partition while I catch my breath.

"What's going on?"

"Someone was following me. So I ran."

I open my eyes to find him smiling wryly, amusement dancing in his eyes. I swat at his chest. "It's not funny!"

"Tall, skinny guy?"

"Yeah…"

"I sent him to keep an eye on you."

I swat him again. "What the hell, Judas? You didn't think to tell me? I thought he was with Nate." My body trembles and he takes a step forward, crowding me against the partition. He's wearing his black shirt with the white dog collar, but now I know who and what he really is, there's something depraved about it. I lift my gaze from the collar to his eyes and his hands press up against the divider, either side of my head. One look at him has my heart stumbling in my chest like a drunk.

"I didn't tell you because I thought we were done."

"And what if I was...am?"

"You're here."

"The church was closer than home," I defend.

That cocky smirk makes an appearance again, and on a priest, it looks wrong, but on him...this true version of him, I realise, it's perfect. "If you feared me, you would have taken your chances."

Reaching up, I cup his jaw. "I'm not scared of you, Judas. Far from it." That's what makes this so conflicting. He leans into my touch before his forehead brushes mine. I should fear him, but maybe my brain just isn't programmed right. I seem to lack fundamental survival instincts. Or perhaps my mind hasn't caught up to the fact that Judas isn't the hero in this story, he's the villain.

"Good."

"Should I though?" I whisper, my fingers now tracing his chin, my thumb skating over his bottom lip. He's so beautiful. So intoxicating. My mind is fighting a losing battle against every other instinctual part of me that simply wants him. No questions asked.

"No. I would never hurt you."

"You're a good man," I say, and I'm not sure whose benefit it's for: his or mine. Can't he be a good man who does bad things?

He laughs at that. "Ah, little lamb, that's just wishful

thinking. I'm not good, but neither are you. Not deep down."
His eyes meet mine, and something passes between us, an
understanding of sorts. I swallow heavily, feeling uncomfortable under his scrutiny like he can see all those ugly
parts of me that I keep buried. But I don't see disapproval or
disgust in his eyes. In a warped way, it feels like a meeting of
kindred souls. Or maybe I'm just trying to justify this twisted
desire I have for him. At this moment, right here, right now,
I'm not sure I care. The repercussions feel meaningless. I
just need him.

I tilt my chin up as if pulled by unseen forces, brushing
my mouth to the corner of his. That spark crackles between
us as one hand creeps through my hair. Tugging, he forces
my head back until his lips can trace the line of my jaw, and
I let him, because the second his lips meet my skin everything else ceases to exist. My body flushes in goosebumps,
my lungs falter, and my heart races. And he's barely even
touched me.

"So responsive," he murmurs against my skin. The grip
on my hair tightens, and his body crushes mine. "You didn't
run, and now I've got you, sweet Delilah." The words sound
like a threat, but I want them to be a promise.

My mind and heart wage war on each other, one
demanding I run from this man, the other praying he never
lets me go.

His mouth slams over mine, and I instantly feel my lip
split open again. I don't care. I want to bleed for him, to
bind us in an unbreakable oath, to be his sacrificial lamb.
A warped little corner of my soul loves the wrongness of it.
The dog collar, the confessional, the depravity...it all
makes my skin prickle with heat and my thighs press
together in anticipation. I want him. All of him. Possessing
me with that darkness that I see in him now. Owning me,

claiming me. Because the devil protects his own, doesn't he?

For one blissful moment, I allow myself to just free-fall into that sweet abyss where it's nothing but this beautiful man and me, and the simple fact that I want him and he wants me.

But reality shoves it's way back into my mind. Guilt whispers in my ear, a familiar old enemy. Isabelle's face flashes through my mind, and my entire body locks down. Placing my hands on his chest, I push him back an inch. He stills, his head falling forward as he sucks in a deep breath.

"I'm sorry," I blurt. His lips twitch, and his knuckles trace delicately over my bruised cheek. "I shouldn't have come here."

He closes the space between us again until every single hard line of him is outlining my softer frame. Lips brush just below my ear, and I shiver as warm breath caresses my skin. "Just let go, Delilah. Stop fighting it."

My fist balls against his hard stomach, the movement sending a sting across my injured palm. "You're bad for me, Judas," I manage.

The coolness of his gaze meets mine. "Yes, I am."

"I...I have to go."

I shove past him, but he catches my arm, holding me against him. "That man will continue to watch you. Don't run from him," he says calmly.

"Judas, I don't need a—"

"Nathaniel will try to approach you at some point. You have the power to destroy him. He will try and make amends in the hope of keeping you quiet." My blood runs cold at the thought, and he nods as though satisfied with my reaction. "Until next time, Delilah." Leaning in, he presses his lips to my forehead, allowing them to linger there.

My fingers grip the front of his shirt as my eyes close. My heart stumbles over itself, hiccupping. "Goodbye, Judas," I breathe.

I move past him and walk out of the church. It hurts. Every step hurts, but what my fragile heart fails to understand is that whatever it may feel, it's not for this man. It's for a lie.

It's late by the time I get home, and the house is plunged in darkness. Turning on the kitchen light, I wrinkle my nose at the state of the place.

There are unwashed dishes in the sink, spilt cereal on the side and a note stuck to the fridge with scrawled sharpie on it.

Lila

Rent is due tomorrow!

Love you. Tiff. X

I snatch it down and dump it in the bin. Damn it. I'd almost forgotten. Taking my phone out, I log in to the Internet banking app and transfer the money. The new balance shows as minus one hundred and thirty pounds and twenty-one pence. Great. Just great. I need a job like yesterday. I wince when my lip stings, and I realise that I've been chewing on it.

Okay, this is shit, but it's controllable. I can get a job. I can fix this. Strangely, I feel a certain power in that. Because of all the crap going on in my life recently, I've had very little control over any of it.

Grabbing a piece of toast, I take it upstairs to my room and open my laptop. I start searching for jobs, any jobs: bar work, weekend retail, even delivery driver positions. I just need something fast. Once I've applied for ten jobs, I close my laptop, lie down and close my tired eyes.

It's pitch black, but I know I'm in the confessional. The scent of wood polish, the sense of confinement, the absolute stillness of the air as it's restricted to a small space. My own breaths are the only sound to echo through the space, and I glance around, waiting. Slowly, my eyes adjust, or perhaps it is getting lighter like the grey light of dawn peaking over the horizon. I make out the silhouette of a figure pressed against the mesh of the divider. Moving closer, I make out the tinge of red hair. My heart rate picks up, and I close my eyes as a tear breaks free.

"You," she says.

"I'm sorry," I whisper.

When I open my eyes, I see a hand at Isabelle's throat, squeezing, choking. She claws at the fingers, her eyes wide.

"No!" I slam my fists against the partition, but it might as well be made of steel.

Out of the darkness, Judas appears over Isabelle's shoulder. A sick grin works over his face as he squeezes her neck harder and harder. Finally, she goes limp, and he drops her.

"We're the same, Delilah," he purrs.

I jolt awake, gasping for air. Just a dream. It was just a dream.

Bright morning sun blinds me, and I hold a hand up, shielding my eyes from it. Dragging myself out of bed, I shower and dress for uni before quickly checking my emails.

There's one new one in my inbox. Subject: When can you start?

Frowning, I open it. It's from Fire Nightclub.

Dear Miss Thomas.

We'd like to offer you a position at our nightclub. We are hosting a grand re-opening event next weekend. Please be at the club at 9.30 p.m. on Friday to go through basic training before your shift.

Regards,

Marcus Manning,
Manager, Fire.

I smile, and relief washes over me. I can't believe I have a job without even having an interview. Finally, something is going right.

The library has that usual eerie silence, the kind that puts you on edge for fear of needing to cough.

I focus on my book, scrawling some notes across the lined paper in front of me. Someone pulls the chair out beside me, and I'm just about to tell them that the seat is taken when I look up and see Judas.

He drops into the chair, his tall, muscular frame filling it to capacity. My eyes dart around the library nervously. Why am I so edgy? It's not like he has drug lord written on his forehead.

It's only been two days since I last saw him, but it feels like forever. I've thought about him constantly. My eyes flick over the charcoal grey suit, his white shirt open at the collar. It all just fits him so well, and suddenly he looks every inch the ruthless businessman, the beautiful, ruthless businessman.

"What are you doing here?" I whisper, forcing my eyes from his accentuated waist and broad shoulders.

"We need to talk. I'm taking you to dinner."

"I told you, I need time."

He lifts a brow. "You've had time. I'm not a patient man."

"How did you know I was here?"

His lips twist up into that wry smile that takes him from good guy to so very bad. His gaze shifts over my shoulder, and I follow it to my own personal stalker. The man looks at Judas, nods, and then simply leaves.

"You know, this is moving into creeper territory," I hiss under my breath.

His smile only deepens, and he leans in, bringing his lips to my ear. "We're way past that."

I shake my head and push to my feet, putting my books in my rucksack. Judas chuckles to himself as he follows me out of the library. He places a hand on my back, leading the way across campus to one of the car parks.

It's not until we've been driving for fifteen minutes that I finally speak.

"Where are we going again?"

"I didn't say."

"Okay. Are you going to tell me?"

"No."

I stare at him. "Are you trying to surprise me?"

He rolls his eyes. "No, I'm just not telling you where we're going."

"That's a surprise."

"No, it's not."

"Fine. Just so you know, I don't like surprises that involve a shovel."

"You think I'd kill you?" A crooked grin shapes his lips.

Truthfully, I don't know anymore. I don't trust my own judgement. It's let me down too many times.

"I think I have a habit of going for bad guys, and my tastes seem to be getting progressively worse." I shake my head, but he has no smart comeback this time.

The soft sounds of a piano drift through the upscale restaurant, the notes trickling over my senses. Candlelight sways back and forth, playing over the golden tones of Judas's skin. I glance around at the dark little corner of the restaurant that he brought us to. We're somewhere outside Covent Garden, and one look at the place tells me I can't afford to be here. Hell, right now I can barely afford McDonald's.

I swirl the olive around in my Martini before bringing it to my lips and prying it from the cocktail stick. Judas's eyes fix on my mouth, his expression darkening.

Sexual tension gives way to anxiety, and I fiddle with the small wooden stick nervously. Judas isn't a priest, and he isn't just running party pills to teenagers. He's a cocaine dealer, a drug lord, a criminal. What I can't work out is why he's pretending to be a priest. So many puzzle pieces are scattered in front of us, waiting to be assembled. But once they are, will I like the picture? I'm not sure there's any way to make that image pretty.

"Why are we here, Judas?" I ask.

"To talk."

I take a sip of my drink, well, more like a hefty gulp, and set the glass back down on the pristine white tablecloth.

"Fine. I don't understand," I say.

"What don't you understand?"

"Any of it."

Our eyes meet across the table, the wavering glow of the candle flickering between us. We say nothing for a moment, but it all hangs right there between us. Words waiting to be said, shots waiting to be fired because once it's all out there, there's no going back. I know it. He knows it. Do we trust each other enough to spill our secrets? Does he trust me? And if he does, am I worthy of that trust?

"Why are you a priest?" He opens his mouth to speak, but I cut him off. "And don't give me the half-cut version. I told you my secrets. I trusted you." He studies me, eyes searching mine, delving deep into the recesses of my self.

"Right now, all I know about you is that you sell drugs." I lower my voice. "Everything rational is telling me to run from you, Judas. As far and as fast as I can. I need you tell me everything." I chew my bottom lip. "I need you to give me a reason to stay."

"And yet here you are, little lamb because whether it's rational or not, you want to be here. You're drawn to me — to this."

I close my eyes for a beat, swallowing down the blind panic that's threatening to consume me as I walk this tightrope that spans the black void of the unknown. He's right. I'm helplessly drawn. I've come to need Judas. When I'm with him, life seems a little more bearable. The guilt of Isabelle's death is still there, but it's muted. He's like a band-aid to everything that's wrong in my life. He makes me feel whole. A little less broken. Stronger. However, he represents the very thing that put me on my knees in the first place. He's been my crutch, but that crutch has grown thorns, and I'm bleeding. Fat crimson drops all over the pristine white of what we once had. There was a certain innocence to it, but now...

"It's not as simple as that, and you know it."

"No?" He hesitates, and I practically choke on my rising heartbeat. "It could be."

The tension breaks when the waitress comes over and places a meat and cheese board down between us. Judas smiles at her politely, and I see the blood rush to her face before she moves away.

"I'm a priest because it was necessary at the time."

"What does that even mean?" I sigh.

"I had to lie low."

"So, what? Now you just run your drug empire from the church?"

"For now. I have people in place to run things for me." His eyes flick up and back down again before he spears a piece of cheese with a cocktail stick and pops it in his mouth. "And the church has its uses."

I absorb those words and lean forward, my voice dropping to a hissed whisper. "You're using the church?" I'm not religious, but even I think there's something sacrilegious about that.

"It's not the most corrupt thing the Catholic faith has done. Don't panic." A small smirk pulls at his lips, and I drop my head into my hands.

"Do you feel guilty, or bad even?"

"For what?"

"You're destroying peoples lives."

"How so? We live in an instant gratification world. People want what they want. There's no morality to it, no sense of risk or failure. I'm a businessman and business is always about supply and demand. Do people take drugs and overdose? Of course. Do they ruin their lives? Often. Can you place that responsibility on the man giving that person those drugs, or on the person taking them? We live in a society where everything is always someone else's fault, especially the man lining his pockets." I shift uncomfortably, not liking the fact that his words make sense.

"If you believe in God though, then you must see that it's wrong." I'm almost begging him, wanting him to say the words I so badly need to hear.

"God tests us, little lamb. I am his test to others. I weed out his sinners. You were your friend's test. She failed."

"No. Drugs killed Izzy." I meet his gaze, tears clinging to my lashes. "And I have to live with that."

Judas sits back in his chair, his eyes narrowed and a cocktail stick resting against his lower lip. He snatches it from his mouth and raps his knuckles on the tabletop. "I can't make that right for you, Delilah. One act does not equal another. You selling those pills is no different to you giving her a bottle of tequila and her then getting behind the wheel and killing herself." He shrugs. "It's piss poor luck. And if you hadn't agreed to deliver those drugs, someone else would. Either way, your friend ends up dead. It's the same story. Call it fate if you like."

I swipe at the tears that have begun trailing down my cheeks in a steady stream. "I feel so guilty all the time." My eyes meet his, so intense, such a beautiful shade of blue. "How can I be okay with this, Judas? You're no better than Nate."

I watch his eyes shutter, his features hardening. Standing up, he tosses some cash down and moves around the table, grabbing my arm, his hold firm but not bruising. Wordlessly, he practically marches me through the restaurant, leaving the untouched platter of food and half-drunk glasses. There's a tension to him that scares me. Outside, a light patter of rain hits the pavement, and a cool breeze sweeps around us, making me shiver. His car is parked in an alley tucked beside the restaurant, and when we reach it, he releases me.

"You think I'm like him?" he asks, his voice quiet, too quiet.

"I...don't know."

"I would never hurt you," he growls.

I hug my arms around myself and lean against the side of the car. "I know, but what you do...you're no better."

"No, I'm not." There's no emotion in his voice, just pure fact. "I am who I am. I sell drugs. I make money. I do bad things. And I want you, Delilah Thomas, as much as you want me." His attention focuses fully on me, and his eyes hone in on my lips. "Tell me to leave you alone." If only I could. Judas moves closer until he's standing right in front of me. "Tell me to stop." Reaching out, he slides his fingers over my neck and into my hair. Warm breath fans over my face and I tilt my chin up, inviting it, needing him. "Tell me you don't want this," he murmurs, closing the small gap between us. His mouth brushes over mine, and my body feels like a live wire, sparking everywhere. My lips part, inviting him in, seeking him out. Accepting my demise. Welcoming his destruction. "I want you, but I won't apologise. I won't ask forgiveness, and I'll never change." Closing my eyes, I place a shaking hand on his chest. Can I do this? Can I accept what he is while hating myself for the same thing? "We're two sides of the same coin, Delilah. Just let go of that morality you cling to so hard."

"I can't," I choke.

"What good has it ever done you? You're an outsider. No one understands you because you aren't like them." His lips whisper over my temple. "But I do because you're just like me."

"I'm not." My voice is nothing more than a fleeting whisper over the pounding of my heart. Fear has my hands trembling and my breaths coming in rapid pants. I'm terrified of his words, scared of the truth.

"You said you feel guilty." His lips brush my ear. "But do you really? Or is it just guilt over the absence of guilt?" *No, he's wrong. He's wrong.* He takes a step back, and a wicked smile dances over his lips as though he can see my mind free falling into the darkness. "You've spent so long pretending that you don't even know yourself anymore. You act how you think you should. You persecute yourself for the simple fact that you don't feel or behave like others."

My heartbeat is so loud it's rattling against my eardrums. "No, I'm not a horrible person!"

"Shh." He rushes forward, his hands cupping my cheeks, thumbs wiping away stray tears. "There's nothing horrible about it. You are who you are, Delilah. Cloaked in shadows. So beautifully steeped in sin." Tipping my face back, he brushes his lips over mine, and I let him. My stupid heart trips over itself and slows like a frightened animal being soothed by its master. Tears continue to fall, covering both our lips. "Dance with me in the dark, little lamb," he whispers, like a demon tempting me to hell. "I'll make you feel so good."

I should resist, but without him, what would I be at this point? This isn't rational or sane. It just is. And the reason it upsets me so much? He's right. I don't know that I feel truly guilty over Izzy's death, and that is where my guilt stems from. I should. I've just passed one off for the other, punished myself because it's all the same, right? But Judas sees. He knows. I don't know that I believe in soul mates, but this inexplicable pull, the way I need him...I could almost believe.

Leaning in, I press my lips to his, clasping his face in my hands. I never want to let go, but I need time to deal with this. Time to think.

"I need time, Judas," I breathe over his lips.

He drags his knuckles over my cheek and down my throat. "Then I'll be waiting."

Cupping my face gently, he places his lips to my forehead. He's warmth and light and safety, and I'm not sure how that is even possible.

"I'll drop you home," he says.

"It's okay. I'll walk."

Pulling away, he moves to the passenger door and pulls it open. "It wasn't a request, Delilah."

He waits for a moment, and I swallow heavily before getting in the car. My head is swimming with thoughts racing through my mind at a hundred miles an hour. My heart aches, letting out choked, pitiful beats within my chest. The ten-minute ride feels like prolonged torture because I know that I'm going to have to get out, and I don't know when I'm going to see him again.

He pulls up outside my house, and I force myself to open the door, refusing to look back. I'm at my front door before I hear the engine rev and pull away. As soon as I'm inside, I release a breath and my body sags.

I already feel like part of me is missing. How has a man I've only know for a few weeks — a man who I really knew nothing about — become so ingrained on me?

It's not right, but does it need to be?

———

A week. It's been a week, and honestly, I imagine this is what a drug addict feels like when they're coming off their habit of choice.

Everything feels so dark, so pointless. I feel like I'm slowly dying.

I knock on the door of the student counsellor's office and wait. "Come in," a voice calls.

Opening the door, I step inside. A middle-aged woman with a sleek brown bob smiles at me from behind her desk. "Hello." She looks down at some papers in front of her, the red-rimmed glasses sliding down her nose as she does. "Delilah Thomas?"

"Yes."

"Good. Sit, sit." She gestures to the seat across from her, offering me a warm smile and bracing her elbows on the desk. "I'm Mary Andrews, the student counsellor here at King's College." I nod in acknowledgement. "Now, tell me why you wanted to see me today, Delilah."

"I'm struggling."

"With your studies?"

"No." I shake my head. "I uh…" God, why am I even here? I can't tell her anything. Yet again that feeling of help-lessness crashes over me. I'm stuck here, forced to endure, unable to move forward, unable to go back. I'm in limbo, and I'm slowly just drifting away.

Suddenly her hand is touching mine, patting over the back of it. "You can tell me anything, Delilah. It will stay between these four walls."

"I…" She smiles, nodding at me to offer encouragement. "My friend died," I blurt. She stills but quickly follows it up with a sympathetic frown.

"I'm sorry. Were you close?"

"Yeah. I feel responsible, unable to move on."

"Why do you think you're responsible?"

I remember Judas analogy, and I realise that I don't have to tell her the whole truth, just some of it. "She was in a car accident. Drink driving. I…I gave her the alcohol," I say.

"I see." She looks at me over her glasses. "And you blame yourself?"

I swallow around the lump in my throat and tears prickle my eyes. "Yes. No. I don't know." I look at her. "I should feel guilty though, right? That's normal."

She gives me a sympathetic look. "Delilah, there are several stages to grief. There is no normal. Everyone handles these things differently. Feeling guilty is to be expected."

I hear the words she doesn't say there. It would be

normal to feel guilty for killing your friend. Of course it would! But I know somewhere along the way I became removed from it because I'm not normal. Just like Judas said.

I push my chair back and stand.

"Thank you for your time. I...I need to go." Grabbing my bag, I whirl for the door.

"Delilah." I pause with my fingers wrapped around the door handle. I hear her release an audible breath. "Be kind to yourself." That's all she says.

I yank the door open and walk outside, the pressure in my chest releasing the second I do. At this point, I'm damned if I do and damned if I don't.

When I get home, I open the fridge and take out the carton of orange juice, pouring a glass. Glancing at the clock, I see that it's nearly seven. It's Friday, and I have to be at Fire for my first shift in a couple of hours.

My phone beeps with a text, so I pick it up, opening the message from an unknown number.

It's a screenshot of a web page. Opening the thumbnail, I skim-read the writing. It's a Companies House business page listing a company called Element Holdings. Why would someone send me this? Zooming in, I keep reading until I pause on a name. The company director is Judas Kingsley. That can't be a coincidence.

Going upstairs, I grab my laptop from where it sits on the bed, the screen showing my current paper. Closing the window, I open the Internet browser, clicking on the search bar.

I type out the name Judas Kingsley and hit enter. Instantly, the page fills with articles, and sure enough, the beautiful face I've come to memorise appears, proving to me that my mind can't do him justice. One of the first things I see is that he owns Fire. Shit. Does he know that Isabelle died in his club? I thought I saw a news report about it being shut down afterwards. How would he feel if he knew I was responsible for that? And did he have anything to do with giving me that job? I push it out of my mind and keep reading like a sponge desperate to soak up everything I can about him.

His father is called William Kingsley, his uncle; Richard Kingsley is running for mayor, and then... I pause on an article on the Telegraph website. There's an image of Judas, a much younger Judas being shoved into a police car, his hands cuffed behind his back. My eyes skim the words, and the more I read, the more horrified I become. I place my hand over my mouth, covering the staggered gasp that slips from my throat. Oh my God, he's a monster.

I don't know him at all.

18

JUDAS

I CHECK my watch and rap my knuckles over the kitchen counter. It's eight in the morning.

Delilah never showed up at the club last night. Which could just be a coincidence. She could have found another job, or just decided against it. But I have a feeling there's more to it. Could she have found out that I own it? Would she be intent enough on staying away from me to turn down employment?

It's been a week since I last saw her. She needed time to come to terms with the truth of who she is, and I thought I could give her that. That I could wait patiently for her to come to me, but it's becoming increasingly harder. I miss those sad eyes, the layer of innocence that tries so desperately to cling to her dark soul.

I still watch her from a distance of course. At home, at university. She looks so lost and broken. If only she would see that I can heal her, that we're two halves of a whole, two black sheep without a shepherd.

I never thought my life was missing anything until this pretty little thing with that broken fucking look wondered into my church. I'm a businessman, a hard man, but she's found a soft spot, and she's dug her claws in. I want to hate her for it, but I can't.

For the first time in my life, I long for something more than money and power, and it makes everything else feel inconsequential. She's blind obsession, and I can't stop.

But she needs a job. I can't help her with many things, but I can help her with that. I worry that she'll crawl back to that parasite of a boyfriend of hers because she's vulnerable, but also because she will seek out the darkness, needing it to balance herself. Nathaniel is like a small bump to a crack addict.

Taking my phone out, I call her, and again she doesn't pick up. Tossing the phone down, I scoop up my keys and leave the apartment.

I make the short drive to her house, the bleak grey drizzle bleeding down my windscreen like tears. When I pull up outside her house, I jog across the road and under the cover of the overhanging porch.

For a moment I stand there, and I want to laugh at the nervous tension sitting in my chest. I'm Judas Kingsley for fuck's sake.

I finally knock, and there's a pause before I hear footsteps and the door swings open. A blonde girl stands there, her eyes wide and her lips slightly parted.

"Uh, hi."

"Is Delilah here?" I ask. She nods mutely before her gaze takes a slow sweep of my body and her teeth sink into her bottom lip. She twirls a strand of hair around her finger.

"Sure. Come in." She steps back, inviting me inside. "Do you want anything to drink?" she asks when we get to the kitchen.

"I just need to see Delilah."

Her expression sours and she rolls her eyes before stepping into the hall. "Lila!" she shouts up the stairs. "There's a guy here for you."

She comes back, hopping onto the kitchen counter and crossing one leg over the other. Her denim skirt rides up her thighs, and her lips tilt into a smirk. I look away from her and fold my arms over my chest.

"Judas." I turn at the sound of Delilah's voice, frowning at the tremor in it.

"Delilah." Her jumper dress hangs off one shoulder, and all I want to do is press my lips to the exposed skin and taste every inch of her. She reminds me of a flower with the purest form of beauty that could so easily be crushed, but instead, I have the urge to caress the softness of its petals, to nurture it. Her full lips are a rosy pink against her pale skin, and I can't help but stare at them. "I need to talk to you."

"Come on." She walks away and up the stairs. I follow her into her room, and she closes the door. The room is simple: a bed, a desk, a chest of drawers. The sheets are pale yellow with white polka dots, and I smile because ever since that day she came to mass, the colour always makes me think of her.

She leans against the windowsill on the far side of the room, her arms folded over her chest and her gaze fixed on the ground.

"Why didn't you take the job?"

She laughs, an edge of hysteria in her voice. "Because you own Fire." Her eyes meet mine. "I know your real name."

"Who I am is irrelevant in this. I'm never at the club. Just take the job." I want to know where she is, to be able to watch her.

She tilts her head back, her eyes falling closed. "I can't work for you, Judas."

I move closer to her until I'm only a couple of feet away. She holds her hand up, freezing me in place. Whatever has happened between us, she's never looked at me the way she is now; like she's scared of me, or disgusted even. It pisses me off.

"Because I'm not the pious priest you thought I was? Because I'm *bad*?" I mock, closing the distance further until her hand presses to my chest. Her fingers curl, nails digging into my skin through my shirt. "Because, let's not forget, prior to your friend's overdose, you were knowingly dating a guy just like me, peddling his drugs without question."

I barely see her move before her palm collides with the side of my face. The sting reverberates over my skin as I swing my gaze back to her.

"There it is." I smile. "Just let it out, little lamb. Let the violence, and the anger take you over."

Tears pool in her eyes before spilling over and running down her cheeks. "You're a fucking monster, Judas! So don't you dare judge me." I blink. A monster? Well, I've been called far worse. "I know!" For a moment I say nothing, but my pulse ticks up.

"Know what?" I ask, but I don't need to. She knows my name. There's only one heinous act that's publically associated with that name.

"Everything!" Her eyes hold mine, the tears continuing to flow. "I know what you did. I know about Brent James." I take a step back away from her and sit on the edge of the bed, giving her space.

"I served my time."

A soft sob breaks from her. "You put him in a wheelchair, Judas."

"Nothing less than he deserves." Her mouth falls open and then snaps shut again as she shakes her head. "The world is not sunshine and rainbows. It's ugly, and sins require punishments."

"You sound insane," she whispers.

"You know nothing."

"Then tell me," she begs. "Make me understand." I see the desperation in her eyes. She's every bit as hooked as I am. She needs justification, to be able to tell herself that I'm not a monster. That way she's not awful for needing me.

"I beat him with a crowbar. He's in a wheelchair, and I was sentenced to ten years for aggravated assault. I became a priest while in prison and only served five for good behaviour." I clasp my hands together in front of me. "That's it. I'm not your Prince Charming, Delilah because the world isn't a fucking fairy tale." I hate that look on her face right now.

I watch the heartbreak in her eyes, the disappointment. "Why did you do it?" I say nothing. I promised Myrina I'd never tell anyone what happened to her, and I haven't. Not when they questioned me, not in front of a jury, and not when I was inside. Would it have helped my case? Maybe. But I'm a man of my word, and I've always had a soft spot for my younger cousin. "Did he steal from you? Drugs? Money?"

That would be logical. Of course, I've hurt and even killed people in the name of business, but this was different. This was unbridled rage. I didn't care about the consequences because I was young and reckless. I attacked him in front of witnesses. "Judas." I blink and look at Delilah. She shakes her head, the light leaving her eyes as though I personally just extinguished it. I've held my tongue for eight long years, but I can't hold it with her.

"He raped my cousin." I won't apologise for what I did because I'm not sorry. "So I beat him to within an inch of his life, and then I stopped." She tilts her head, her brows knitting together. "I could have killed him, but I wanted him to suffer." I lay it all out there. Allow her to see the twisting, writhing demons dancing around in fire and brimstone behind my eyes. "And now he is. Every day."

"I'm—"

I push to my feet and smooth a hand over the front of my shirt. "If you want that job, be at the club tonight. Nine thirty."

I walk towards the door, my muscles tense and my fists clenched at my sides. I can feel her judgement, and it pisses me off more than I can say.

"Judas," she says, and I pause. "I'm sorry."

"So am I."

The club is packed wall to wall. It seems a shut down due to an overdose only makes a place more popular these days. The queue extends around the block, and the bar is five-deep with people waiting for drinks.

My club manager, Marcus, wanted a big re-opening weekend to draw the crowds. It's Saturday night, and the theme is Purge. Tattered material hangs from the ceiling, covered in fake blood like a house of horrors. Steel-barred cages have been placed in the centre of the dance floor, and girls dance both in and on them, wearing tight shorts, combat boots and ripped up tanks. Balaclavas cover their faces, the eyes X'd out. Fire dancers move across the top of the DJ booth where some new hotshot rapper is drawing a crowd. And from my office, I can see straight across the club to the VIP area, set on three, tiered balconies. My eyes hone in on the top tier, the table of people laughing and flirting, sipping champagne. Delilah walks over to them, presenting a bottle of vodka, a sparkler glistening in the top. Every man at the table pays attention to her because they can't physically help themselves.

One of the girls dressed her, and fuck, I wish I'd told them to keep her covered up. She's wearing black denim shorts that are so small and tight that half her arse is on show. Fishnet tights cover the length of her thigh between the shorts and knee-high combat boots. Her ripped up white tank is tied up at the bottom and torn at the top exposing both her stomach and her cleavage. She's like every man's wet dream, with all that on display and her bright-as-sunshine smile that hides so much tragedy.

I hate that their eyes are on her, but my eyes are on her as well. One wrong move and their bodies will be washing up on a riverbank a few miles down the Thames.

She delivers the bottle, and one of the guys tries to slip some cash into the waistband of her shorts. She ducks away taking the money from his hand with a polite smile. She's fresh meat with an air of naivety about her. They sense it. They want it — to defile and destroy. Isn't that human nature? To take and desecrate beautiful things?

I force my gaze away from her, my eyes sweeping across the floor of the club, but I pause when I see a familiar figure. Nathaniel. I wonder if he's unaware I own the place, or if he just likes to dance with death.

He's talking to a girl — their heads bent close as they huddle against the back wall. I take the radio from my jacket pocket.

"Jackson, there's a girl. Back wall. Blonde. Blue dress. Search her. Wait until she moves away from the guy."

"Yes, sir." His voice crackles through the speaker.

I open my office door, stepping out into the sensory overload that is the club. Metal steps lead down behind the bar, and I jog down them, keeping an eye on Nathaniel through the crowd. The club is so packed I can barely move, but I spot him, talking to a guy this time. He's young, probably eighteen, a student. They slap hands, and there's the unmistakeable shady hug of a drug exchange. I would know. They part ways, and the guy walks straight towards me. Just as he gets beside me, I grab the front of his shirt, tugging him close as I shove my free hand in his jeans pocket, pinching the small plastic bag of pills.

"Leave, before I have you arrested."

He staggers away from me; his face washed white. I barely spare him a fleeting glance before I move on, following Nathaniel. As he passes the door that leads to the basement, I move. Striding up to him I grab him by the back of the neck and slam his cheek to the door.

"What the fuck," he spits, but the music is loud, too loud for anyone to hear his struggle, and even if they do, they're too drunk to react quickly. I swipe my key card over the lock, and it opens, allowing us to spill into the corridor beyond.

He staggers, but quickly straightens, taking a swing at me. Ducking, I crack my neck and punch him square in the throat.

"I told you to stay away."

He grasps his knee with one hand, clutching the casted one to his chest. He coughs and chokes, dragging in stilted breaths. His face is still a map of blues and purples from our last run in, and his nose is definitely not straight any more. "And yet, here you are, in my club. Dealing." I squeeze my fist, the knuckles giving out a satisfying crack.

"You said..." Another wheezing cough. "Not to come near *her*."

I drag him to his feet and ram him up against the wall by his throat. "You're here. She's here. I'd say that's near, wouldn't you?"

"How was I to know that? I do come for the hot girls though, and Delilah is hot." He lets out a raspy laugh. My grip on his neck tightens. "A good fuck too."

My temper spikes viciously, and I want to drive my fist into his face until his skull caves in and his body goes limp. Instead, I simply squeeze, tighter, tighter. He wheezes, his mouth opening and closing and his fist thumping against my body, but it does nothing. The blood vessels in his eyes burst, the red exploding over the white in a way that's so satisfying. I'm vaguely aware of the sound of the door opening.

"Judas!" I blink, breaking the stare-down I have going on with Nathaniel's bloodshot eyes. A small hand lands on my face, pulling me, forcing me to turn my head until I'm looking at Delilah. Her brows are pulled together tightly, but her eyes are...sympathetic?

"Judas, let him go." My grip remains, and I can feel his pulse slowing under my fingers. She strokes my cheek.

"He hurt you, Delilah."

She nods. "I know, but—"

"Just say the word, little lamb."

She hesitates, her gaze flicking to Nathaniel. He's starting to sag in my grip. I can see the possibilities flicking through her mind. "There are cameras," she whispers. "Witnesses who saw you come in here." Ah, but she wants him dead. She simply fears the consequences.

"Doesn't matter."

Her gaze strays back to me, eyes softening as she places her hand on my arm. "Not here.

Just let go for me." Slowly, my fingers respond, releasing his neck. He falls to the ground in a heap, sucking in huge gulps of air.

"I warned him," I explain, my voice not as steady as I'd like. Rage courses through my veins, spiking my adrenaline until it's all I can do to remain planted in front of her.

"I know." Her fingers brush my lips, nails scratching over my jaw. "But I'm not letting you go back to prison. You have to let him walk out of here."

I want him dead, but I'm not going to pull the trigger for her. This needs to be her decision. Nathaniel is her problem, and there will come a time when she can handle him. I have to let her so she can blossom into everything that she's meant to be.

There's a hacking, choked laugh from behind me, and I close my eyes, grinding my teeth over each other.

"What, you didn't fancy fucking a dealer anymore, Delilah? Thought you'd move up the food chain?" Nate rasps.

"Shut the fuck up," I growl.

He takes a step toward Delilah, and she flinches back, pressing herself to my side as though I'll protect her from the big bad monster. And I will. Always.

"Does he know?" Nathaniel sneers. "That it was you who killed Isabelle? Here. In his club. It was you who got him shut down." Delilah's nails dig into my arm, and she drops her head, allowing her hair to blanket her face. "Enjoy it while it lasts, baby. When he's done with you, I'll be waiting."

I step forward, but she tightens her grip, latching onto my arm. "Let him go," she whispers.

"Tick tock, Nathaniel. It's only a matter of time," I say with a smile.

As soon as he walks out of the door, Delilah releases me and steps back. Her hands cover her face, and her shoulders tremble.

"Hey." I sweep her hair behind her ear, and she slowly lowers her hands from her tear-stained face.

"I can't do this anymore," she chokes. "I'm not this person, Judas! I'm not the girl caught between rival drug dealers and getting beaten up by her boyfriend, or...or..." She breaks down, sagging against the wall.

I pull her to me, wrapping my arms around her small body. She's breaking, and it's so precious because as she splinters apart, she'll reform into something stronger. Every time her conscience and morality plague her like this, she gets just a little further from them. She's driving herself right into my arms, and I don't have to do a single thing.

I'll be her white knight with dark intentions.

"I shouldn't do this with you," she sniffs.

"What would you have me do? Walk away and leave you to the wolves."

"You are the wolf, Judas," she breathes, burying her face against my chest.

I stroke over the length of her hair and drop my lips to her ear. "But I'm your wolf, little lamb."

A choked sound leaves her lips and her arms wind around my back, fingers gripping handfuls of my suit jacket. She holds on like I'm her lifeline, and my heart thumps unevenly in response. Long moments of silence stretch between us, and I press my lips to her hair, inhaling the sweet vanilla scent that I've missed so much.

"I'm sorry," she whispers. "I should have told you that it was me, that is was here..."

"Delilah. I knew the second you told me what you did."

"Aren't you supposed to kill me or something?" she sniffs. "For messing with your business."

"You've been watching too much Godfather."

Backing away, she lifts a trembling hand, dragging it through her hair. Her fingers grip the strands, pulling hard enough that I'm sure she wants the little sting of pain. Her makeup is streaked down her face in despairing lines like she's melting away.

"Come on, let's go." I offer her my hand, and she stares at it for a moment. "I'm not going to hurt you, Delilah."

Her gaze lifts from my hand to my face, eyes filled with unshed tears. When I first met her, I thought she looked so beautifully broken but so innocent. I wanted to ruin her, and I think that maybe I finally have. Now I'll unleash her.

"Trust me," I practically beg.

"No more secrets?" she whispers.

"No more secrets."

On a deep breath, she places her hand in mine, and I tug her forward, leading her down the hallway to the fire exit at the end. When I shove it open, an alarm starts blaring, but I don't care. My car sits in the car park only a few feet away.

She says nothing as I drive through the London traffic to Hammersmith. The silence in the car brings with it a certain finality. Our secrets are all out, and they're ugly and twisted, but we're here. She's here, which means she's accepted the depravity she knows I'll bring. She's finally succumbing to it.

Once inside my apartment, I go and find an oversized t-shirt and a pair of workout shorts, tossing them to her where she sits on the couch. "You can wear that." She looks between the garments beside her and me, her brows furrowing in confusion. "More for my benefit," I say.

"You want me to cover up?" she asks, and fuck, she sounds so innocent.

I force myself to remain rooted here, across the other side of the room. My eyes roam over her long legs, the exposed skin of her stomach, her tits straining against the confines of that ripped up tank. Fuck no, I don't want her to cover up.

I groan and drag a hand down my face. "Delilah."

She pushes to her feet, her head tilting to the side and spilling waves of shiny dark hair over her shoulder. "You said no more secrets."

She moves closer. "It's not a secret that I want you, little lamb." My eyes are fixed on her chest, my dick hardening with every step she takes, each lethal swing of those hips.

"Judas." My eyes snap to her face, and she blushes, her gaze dropping to the floor for a moment. I love how unsure of herself she is, that she still doubts this hold she seems to have over me. "I'm done fighting this."

19

DELILAH

JUDAS LINGERS across the other side of the room, his expression guarded and his body tight with tension. His hands are shoved deep in the pockets of his black trousers, and his forearms are roped in veins, exposed by the rolled up sleeves of his shirt. A muscle in his jaw ticks against his skin, and I can practically time my heartbeats to it.

"I'm done fighting this." Four words. Four words that change everything. I'm taking a sledgehammer to this wall that I've forced between us because I don't care anymore. Everything is out in the open now. He knows what I did, the deepest, darkest parts of me. I know what he did, and I know why.

"You're still wary of me," he says, taking a slow step towards me.

I nod because I won't lie to him. "I'm scared of who I am when I'm with you." A girl without morals. A girl who sees things that were once wrong, as acceptable.

"Don't be. She's the real you, the one you hide from everyone else. But you can't hide from me." A small predatory smile works over his lips.

"I don't want to."

He closes the remaining distance, stroking his fingers over my cheek as his eyes land on every inch of my face, studying me. "Be sure about this, Delilah. I'm not the sort of guy you change your mind with. I won't just let you go."

"I don't want you to let go," I say on a shaky breath.

He moves at the same time as I do, our bodies colliding and our lips sealing together. He steals my breath. He steals every part of me until I feel like I exist solely for him. His arms enclose around my waist, shielding me from the world, and I've never felt so safe, so cherished. I want every part of him. I want to be possessed and branded, for him to always want me, to always keep me safe. He's my wolf. My tamed savage.

My fingers fumble with the fastenings of his shirt until I lose patience and yank the material apart. The buttons scatter across the wooden flooring like fat raindrops of inhibition tinkling to earth. Grasping my waist, he wrenches me off the floor and tosses me on the sofa. I watch him like a hawk as he unfastens his trousers and pushes them and his underwear down. Heat creeps into my cheeks and then spreads over my entire body. He truly is the most beautiful thing I've ever seen, and I decide right then and there that Judas should never wear clothes.

He peels my clothing off, one painful item at a time until I'm panting in anticipation. His stare alone makes me feel worshipped in the most reverent of ways.

He tugs me from the sofa cushions and sits, forcing me into his lap. Warm skin brushes mine, and that static current that always seems to exist between us crackles to life in full force. Cupping my face, he presses his lips to mine in a way that steals my breath and has my heart galloping in my chest. I expect rough and brutal. I expect to be torn apart from the inside out. I expect his destruction, but as he slides inside me, it's like he's collecting all the fractured little pieces of me, and keeping them safe.

My forehead touches his, and our heavy breaths intermingle. That dark corner of my soul sighs in relief — like its found a balance — like its finally been accepted.

"You feel like heaven, Delilah," he breathes against my mouth. And then his hands are on my hips, forcing me over him, contorting my body like a puppet master. I don't recognise the sounds falling from my own lips, or the way my nails rake over the skin of his chest. I'm possessed...by him.

"Look at me," he demands, and my eyes snap open, meeting his. So intense, so full of desire. He drags his thumb over my bottom lip before he leans in and nips it. "You're so beautiful like this," he groans.

It's too much. He's too much. My lungs strain for air and my pulse is hammering so loud that it's ringing against my ears.

His arms slide up my back, biceps locking either side of my waist as his fingers wind into my hair. My head is wrenched back, my spine bowing and my body allowing him deeper. Soft becomes hard. Tender becomes brutal, and I welcome it because I want the storm that is Judas. I want lashing rain and howling wind. I want to have my foundations shaken and ripped up. I need him to pull me from the wreckage and allow me to be reborn: stronger, better.

His teeth sink into the tender skin of my neck, marking and claiming. He takes everything I have to give, and I offer it freely, hoping that he'll care for those little pieces he's holding. Knowing that if I just surrender, he'll glue me back together.

I cling to him, riding out the storm with him, his name falling from my lips like a prayer.

"Break for me, sweet Delilah," he rasps.

My body tightens and pleasure tears through me so hot and fast that my vision dots and my head spins, and all those little pieces he's holding: he scatters them to the wind. He watches me crumble to dust before his eyes and replaces everything I once was... with him, until he infects every cell, every breath, every thought.

A feral growl sounds from his throat and Judas stills beneath me. Wrenching me forward, he holds me against him and touches his forehead to mine. Hard breaths wash over my face.

"So beautiful." His hands cup my face, thumbs swiping below my eyes, catching stray tears that I didn't even know were there. "So pretty when you cry," he whispers over my lips.

Releasing me, he throws his head back against the couch, his chest rising and falling on heavy breaths. His lashes cast shadows over his cheeks and full lips part as he sucks in deep breaths. I'm still staring at him when his eyes flash open, and he lifts his head. Fingers trail over my stomach, making me shiver and flush with goosebumps. The steady thrumming of my heart pounds against my eardrums so loud that I'm sure he must be able to hear it.

This isn't just sex. This is something else entirely. He said he wouldn't let me go, and I feel it. I feel like I'm splitting apart for him, inviting him to live inside me.

"You're mine now, Delilah. There's nowhere you can hide. I see you."

. . .

I nod, feeling the vulnerability, sensing the change in the air. I just gave Judas Kingsley the power to break me entirely, but I know he won't because he's my salvation.

I shower and step into Judas's room, finding some clothes left out on the bed. Smiling, I tug the soft material of the t-shirt over my head and step into the boxers. Then I go in search of him.

He's in the kitchen, his hip propped against the counter and his phone in his hand as he types something out on the screen.

A pair of joggers rides low on his hips, and I can't help but stare. He's just tanned skin, and ink, and muscle. So much muscle. I could truly believe he is the devil because how can one man have a body like that coupled with a face so perfect? I'm sure it defies some kind of mortal law. It takes me a second to realise he's stopped typing. When I meet his gaze, a cocky smile dances over his lips, and he folds his arms over his chest. He takes me in slowly, and I blush, fidgeting on the spot.

Pushing off the counter, he stalks toward me, sliding his fingers beneath the hem of the boxers and cupping my arse. "I like you in my clothes," he murmurs against my ear, making me shiver. He moves past me, and I glance over my shoulder at him. "Help yourself to anything you want," he says before leaving the room.

. . .

I hear the shower start just as I open the fridge, spotting the bottle of white wine. I pour myself a glass and sit at the breakfast bar, taking several large gulps as I think of the gravity of my new situation. Maybe I should be scared, to be so consumed with a man like Judas...but I'm not. It feels right.

I jump when fingers glide over my waist. "That bad?" Judas laughs, the sound a low rumble.

I turn on the stool and hold the glass of wine up. "You make me nervous," I blurt.

"I know." His teeth scrape over his bottom lip in a half smile. "Come on." He tugs me off the stool and leads me to the couch, sitting and pulling me into his lap. I clutch my wine between us like a weapon, and he laughs, plucking it from my hand and taking a sip before he places it on the side table.

"You're supposed to be nervous." His hand drops to my chest, and he places it over my heart. "That nervous titter in your stomach, the racing of your heart; its survival instinct. It's your mind telling you to run."

. . .

"But my heart won't let me run from you, Judas." I tried. I did.

His lips twitch. "Because it knows."

"Knows what?"

He lifts his hand, brushing his knuckles down my cheek. His eyes take in every detail of my face as though committing it to memory. "That you're mine. That we're the same, you and I." The little knot of anxiety in my stomach releases slightly. He kisses my forehead. "I told you. I won't let you go, Delilah."

I wind my arms around his neck and press my lips to his. This desperate debilitating feeling wraps around my heart, squeezing tight.

"I love you, Judas," I confess on a whisper.

A small smile touches his lips, and a certain peace washes over his features. "Only a tainted soul would love the damned."

I don't want to move. I'm warm and comfortable with Judas's chest beneath my cheek and his arms around me. The heavy thump, thump, thump of his heart is like its own melody.

Reaching up, I trail my fingers lazily over his chest, and after a few moments, I realise there are bumps on his skin. Not bumps, lines. Pitching up on my elbow, I glance down at his chest, pressing my fingers to the lines that are cleverly hidden amongst the angel's wings, but there nonetheless. When I look closer, I see they are a tally.

"Scars," Judas murmurs.

I meet the clear blue of his gaze. He's watching me intently. "From what?"

"A knife." He smooths his palm over his pec. "One mark for every sin."

My eyes widen, and I look at the marks from a different perspective. "There are hundreds. Judas, that's…"

"A lot. I know. My brother and I have been accruing them since we were ten years old." I notice one that disrupts the ink rather than being embedded in it. The skin is a faded pink line through the black. I brush my finger over it. "A newer one."

"Why?"

"Our dad was a gangster, our ma was a borderline cult Catholic, and my brother is a psychopath. Saint thought it was better for his sins to mar his body rather than his soul. I just went along with it because it meant I got to take a knife to my brother." Dear God, how messed up is his family?

"Wait, so you do believe in God?"

He smirks. "Is that so hard to believe?"

"Uh, you're a drug dealer, Judas. Yes."

"Are a man's occupation and his faith mutually inclusive?"

"You're turning this into a conversation on morality?"

"I believe in God. I just don't believe quite in the same way that others do."

.   .   .

"So, what? You have a private agreement with him?"

A grin stretches his face. "Something like that."

"You have to give me more than that, Judas. You're cutting sins into your chest, dealing drugs from a church. Don't they say that to go against the church is to go against God?"

"Well, the bible would have you believe that the world is black and white. Good and evil. God and The Devil. But there's always darkness in light." He sweeps my hair away from my face, fingers trailing delicately over my skin. "You're the perfect example of that, Delilah. Such depravity amongst so much purity."

"So you're both?"

"No. I told you before. God tests us. Think of me as a trial on the path of life."

"Or a demon trying to lead people into sin."

His lips twitch. "Or that."

.   .   .

"By your theory, I think I failed my test." I brush my finger-tips over his full lips, so perfect, so kissable. "I'm going to hell."

He leans in, kissing below my ear. "I'll tell you a secret. All the best people are."

"Now you're just stealing lines from Lewis Carol." I laugh. "Were you religious...before?"

"I didn't find Jesus in prison, Delilah. That's so cliché."

"Oh, I'm sorry I don't know the etiquette for going to prison and coming out a priest. Pretty sure that's not normal."

"No, but it got me five years off my sentence." Another smile. "How can anyone dispute that a priest has repented and changed his ways?"

"Oh my God, you're the devil."

A laugh bubbles up his throat. "It wasn't hard. I spent years going to church, listening to bible verses and sermons. Ma made us read the good book before bed every night."

. . .

"Wow."

"Yep."

"But you're still a priest now…"

"The last thing I need is police looking at me too closely. The Kingsley name isn't exactly clean."

"Wait, they know about you?"

He snorts. "My father and uncle have run this city since the eighties. Everyone knows what we do, but no one can prove it. Even though my charges were nothing to do with the family business, they were still unwanted attention."

I nod. "And your cousin?"

He meets my gaze. "Is fine. No one knows what happened to her."

"No one?"

.   .   .

He shakes his head, his eyes hardening. "Her, me, him, and now you."

I swallow heavily. "I'm sorry," I whisper. "I didn't mean to pry, I..."

"I told you because I wanted to, Delilah. When I was arrested, they all looked at me like I was an animal. The Kingsley who beat a twenty-year-old kid into paralysis. And I never gave a shit. Never thought I would. Until you looked at me like that."

I chew my bottom lip, not sure what to say. "I'm under no illusions as to who you are, Judas, but you're not an animal. I wish...I wish there were someone in my life who would go to such lengths for me. Your cousin is very lucky."

He brings my hand to his lips. "I would go to those lengths for you, Delilah." My heart misses a vital beat before tripping into a loping gait again.

His eyes meet mine, holding my gaze. Everything sits right there on his face, though no words are spoken. Some things are beyond words.

20

JUDAS

I STAND AT THE SINK, brushing my teeth and staring in the fogged-over mirror at the perfection of Delilah's form. She tosses her head back, allowing the water to caress her body. She's like art. It's been a week since she broke for me. Two weeks since everything changed, and each day she descends just a little further into my arms, further into the darkness — because the two are mutually inclusive. That person she once was is a fleeting memory, ever shrinking, and in her acceptance, she's found peace. The chaos in her eyes has dimmed, and the sadness that used to define her is but a whisper in her mind. I love to watch her twist and writhe as she transforms from an innocent caterpillar into a butterfly on shadowy wings.

Spitting in the sink, I rinse and walk out of the room before I'm tempted to get in that shower with her. We have work to do today.

The shower cuts off, and a few seconds later she steps into the bedroom with a towel wrapped around her. She eyes the garments on the bed, wrinkling her nose.

"You got me workout clothes?"

I knew she'd complain. "Just put them on."

"Don't you have to go to church today?"

"Day off."

"You have days off?"

"Yes."

She frowns. "But you're always there."

"Only for you."

"What do you mean?" she breathes. Ah, she gravely underestimates my obsession.

I move behind her and sweep the wet hair from her neck, grazing her soft, milky skin with my fingertips. "So I could hear your confession."

She tilts her head to the side, allowing me to kiss her throat. "But why?"

"Because I needed it. Because you needed it. Because you've always been my lost little lamb, just waiting to be found." She turns in my arms, her eyes meeting mine. I sweep my fingers over the heated skin of her cheek. "Does that scare you?"

"No," she breathes. She likes it. I can see it in her eyes. She loves my obsession because it counters her own. We're the reflection of each other — both standing at the glass, pressing our palms to it, trying to crawl inside the other.

"All your sins are mine."

"Everything is yours, Judas." Pushing up on tiptoes, she brushes her lips over mine, so gentle, so sweet.

"Good. Now get dressed."

She groans. "I don't do physical activity."

I trail my fingers up her thighs and under the towel, slowly parting it. "Well, that's not true." Her skin flushes, and I force my eyes to remain on her face as I graze my fingers over her stomach. "You can be very physical." Her breath hitches, her lips parting, and when I lean in, she sways towards me like she's drunk. "Get. Dressed," I murmur against her ear.

"You're a horrible person."

"I'm aware," I call as I walk out of the room.

I'm sitting at the breakfast bar clutching a mug of coffee when she walks in. And damn, those leggings look good on her. For a girl who doesn't do physical activity, she is blessed.

I thrust a to-go coffee mug in her hand and stand, heading for the door. She wordlessly follows me all the way down to the gym in the basement of the building. No one ever uses it aside from me, and it's empty.

She glances around, wrinkling her nose. "Do you think I'm fat or something?"

"No, I think you're scared." The look of disgust turns to confusion.

"What?"

"You're scared of Nathaniel." She swallows heavily, her shoulders becoming tense. She tries to stay at mine almost every night if she can, and though I know she's every bit as consumed with this as I am, it's not that. She's scared that he'll find her. At first, I was simply going to kill him, but, this is her demon, and only she can slay it. "Why are you scared?"

"Because you can't always be there, Judas."

"My name alone should be enough to protect you, but Nathaniel...this is about more than business for him. So, I'm going to teach you how to defend yourself."

She shuffles awkwardly on her feet. "This is going to hurt, isn't it?"

I smile. "I'll go easy on you, little lamb. Basics: eyes, throat, crotch. Hit any of them, and then you run."

I show her, and her brows knit together in concentration

as she copies everything I do. She's a tiny little thing, but after an hour or so, she's really quite good.

I dive towards her, and she swerves, bringing her fist to my throat with more force than I was expecting. I cough, and her face goes pale.

"Oh my god, I'm sorry."

I laugh. "You don't apologise for getting me, Delilah."

I step back, and to the left, she intuitively counters to the right, like an enchanted snake dancing to my tune. She gets me three more times before we stop.

"Now I have something for you."

I slide my hand into the pocket of my tracksuit bottoms and take out the knife that I bought for her. Initially, it looks inconspicuous. Only the handle is visible, made of ornate wood and inlaid with silver. When I pull the blade out, her eyes widen.

"You want me to carry a knife?"

"It'll make you feel better."

She cautiously takes it from me, staring at the small blade in her hand. "Do you really think Nate will come after me?" she whispers.

"I think you should always be prepared. Now—" I take her hand, folding the blade away. "I'm going to come at you. Instead of avoiding me, step into it, pull me close and thrust the knife toward my stomach."

We do it again, and again, and again until I see that little light in her eye, the lust for power; the willingness to draw blood.

"Good." I kiss her forehead, inhaling the scent of vanilla, mixed with her sweat.

"Thank you," she breathes, lifting her chin and glancing up at me through those endless lashes. Her mouth presses to mine, lingering long enough to make my fingers tighten on her waist and wrench her forward. My tongue sweeps over her bottom lip, and she moans like the little demon she is, enticing me beyond the realms of control.

Ah, my sordid sinner. She's intoxicating. I'll willingly bury myself in her and call it salvation.

I stand outside the church with that fake smile plastered on my face, the same way I do every Sunday. The parishioners all file past me, shaking my hand and smiling as though God himself is touching them.

"Judas." I turn at the sound of the distinctive Irish accent barking my name. I instinctively cringe like I'm in trouble.

My mother marches up to me, her pale pink dress and cream lace jacket making her look more like she's attending a wedding than church.

"Ma, I wasn't expecting you."

She yanks me into a hug and kisses my cheek, no doubt leaving her pink lipstick on my cheek. Her grey-streaked red hair is a mass of curls that are always completely wild, no matter what she does. I can't imagine my mother ever looking truly put together. It wouldn't suit her. Dad always jokes that her hair was the Lord's warning that she's mental.

"Well, you'd know if ya ever picked up ya phone," she snaps. "Haven't heard a dickie bird in weeks."

"I've been busy." With Delilah.

She narrows her eyes. "Aye, doing the devil's work." Here we go. "I don't know how you can serve the Lord Almighty in one breath and feed the devil with the next." She shakes her head in disappointment, and I want to bash my head against the nearest wall.

"Ma, why don't you go inside and take a seat? I didn't

reserve one though because I didn't know you were coming." She lifts her chin and strolls past me into the church. I know she's about to kick some old lady off the front pew without an ounce of shame.

Sure enough, when I get up on the pulpit, there's my mother, pride of place, right in the front.

"The Lord be with you," I say.

There's the groaning of the hinges as the huge church door opens. I'm surprised to see Delilah slip through and take a seat in the back pew. She's wearing a scarlet red dress, and I smile. I remember the first time she came to mass in her little yellow dress, looking like sunshine and innocence. She's changed, morphed. Now she sits there like the little sinner she is in blood red, as though she were the Devil's own personal representative. There's an air around her, the shameful confidence of a sinner who does not seek forgiveness. She's beautiful. She's perfect.

I go through the motions of Mass, reading prayers and sermons. Finally, it's time for communion. I opt to do the bread again because I don't want Father Daniel's fingers anywhere near Delilah's mouth. My mother is the first one, of course, shouldering everyone else out of the way. She falls to her knees in front of me, bowing her head reverently.

"The body of Christ." I place the bread on her tongue, and she takes it, crossing herself.

"Amen."

Then she's up and heading for the wine. Her favourite part.

The entire congregation passes by, and exactly the same as before, Delilah waits until the very end.

"Get on your knee's, little lamb," I whisper. A wry smile pulls at her lips, and she falls to her knees easily, keeping her eyes fixed on my feet. "Look at me." She looks up through her lashes, so pretty, so devious. "Open." Her lips part and my cock twitches in response. I place the bread on her tongue, and she closes her lips around my fingers, her teeth scraping the pad of my thumb before her tongue swipes over it. My cock turns to stone, and I fight back a groan.

"I think you're supposed to say something," she prompts with a smug smirk.

"The body of Christ," I grate out.

"Amen."

She stands up, her head bowed, everything about her appearing suddenly demure. Fuck. It's a good job these robes hide everything.

I hurry through the rest of the service, my eyes continually straying to Delilah. By the time I'm finished, I'm ready to toss everyone out and lock the doors.

People linger outside the church, and Father Daniels goes out to play friendly neighbourhood priest. He actually is though. I spot my mother talking to Mrs Jones, no doubt about their book club. Dad says all they do is drink wine and read porn. That's got to be worth at least three Hail Marys.

I should go out there, but Delilah is still sitting on that back pew, one leg crossed over the other as she reads one of the bibles. I move to the end of her pew and stop.

"What are you doing?"

She looks up. "Waiting for you."

Grabbing her hand, I tug her to her feet. I force myself to release her and place a hand on her back as I walk towards the rear of the church. Just in case anyone is looking. As soon as I get her in the office, she's shoved up against the door.

"You think it's funny to give me a hard-on in church?"

Her teeth scrape over her bottom lip, and she shoves her chest forward until it brushes against me. "I did what you told me. Got on my knees, looked at you, opened my mouth..."

Grabbing her waist, I tug her away from the door and throw her down on the desk. Her dress rides up, showing the black lace of her underwear. She pushes up onto her hands, bringing her lips to mine.

"I missed you," she breathes against my mouth.

"I fucking missed you." I had to take a couple of days and meet with new distributors. I almost took her with me because even though it's been weeks, I don't trust that Nathaniel or his bosses won't make a move. However, as much as I long to corrupt, Delilah, I don't wish to make her known to anyone who may be seeking a weakness. She doesn't need to be in my world.

She kisses me, her lips soft and warm, compliant and willing. My fingers go to her hair as her palms cup my jaw. And then a throat clears behind me.

Tearing away from Delilah, I turn around, standing in front of her and blocking her from view. My mother stands there with a raised eyebrow and her arms folded over her chest.

"Fucking hell, Ma. You couldn't have knocked?"

"Judas Moses Kingsley, you wash that blasphemy out of your mouth." There's a snort of laughter behind me before it cuts off. "Why would I knock? Not like I expect the priest to be in here fornicating."

I roll my eyes. "It's me. Your expectations should be low."

She tries to peer around me to Delilah. "You shouldn't be taking advantage of some poor lass."

I groan and toss my head back, praying for strength.

Stepping aside, I reveal Delilah, hoping to God that her skirt is no longer up around her hips. "Ma, this is Delilah."

Delilah sits on the desk, one leg crossed over the other. Her cheeks stained a deep red as she smiles shyly at my mother. "Hi. It's nice to meet you."

Ma offers her a smile, no, *that* smile; the 'I'm a good Catholic, and I'll save you from my heathen son smile. "You seem like a nice lass. Young. Pretty." She flashes me a judgemental look like I just kidnapped a virgin for a satanic sacrifice. "I love my boy, but if I were you, I'd steer clear."

"Ma!"

"He may be a man of God, and he's a good boy, but he's a helpless sinner."

Fuck me. Really? "She's aware. Now, I'll call you." I kiss her cheek and shuffle her towards the door.

"No, come for dinner this evening!"

"I'll call you." I slam the door and brace my back against it. Delilah erupts in laughter. "Yeah, laugh it up."

"I don't know whether to be mortified or amused. She's great."

Fucking hell, if there's one thing that never needed to happen, it was for Delilah to meet my mother or any of my family.

21

DELILAH

Days seem to blend into weeks, and life takes on a new normal. I work at Fire. I go to uni. I see Judas, and he's become more of a salvation than I could ever have predicted. He's not a band-aid anymore, he's become the very cells that knit together and seal all my wounds. He's part of me, so ingrained that to lose him would be like tearing my heart from my body and willing it to still beat. He makes me embrace myself and let go of all the things I was clinging to, all the things that made feel like I wasn't good enough. I've accepted that maybe I'm not good. It terrifies me every bit as much as it thrills me.

I step out of the back room at Fire with a fresh bottle of vodka. As soon as I open the door into the main club, the music pounds through my body, vibrating my bones. The tiny leather shorts I'm wearing ride up my arse, and I'm conscious of the lingering stares aimed my way. Judas hates it. He's tried to make me work in the office, or just cover up more, but there's a reason the VIP girls earn so much money. He knows it as well, hence why he has them wear the outfits in the first place.

The bouncers at the bottom of the stairs part, allowing me through to the VIP bar. I open the bottle and clip a sparkler to the top, lighting it. As soon as I walk over to the table, there's a cheer of applause from the rowdy guys that I've been serving all night. They're obnoxious, but they've already tipped several hundred tonight, and there's still hours before close.

A couple of the guys lean into each other, wide grins on their faces as one talks into the other's ear. Their eyes sweep the length of my legs, and I fix my face into an expression of cool indifference. Too many smiles and they start to wonder just what you're prepared to do for the good tips.

I place the bottle in the ice bucket and bend over the low table, removing the sparkler from the top. I feel the brush of fingers on the back of my thigh, and as I straighten, a hand grabs my arse, wrenching me forward. I stumble, my knee landing on the couch beside one of the drunken guys, my crotch in his face.

"I suggest you let me go."

"Aw, come on baby," he slurs. "Haven't we been nice to you all night?"

"We have, Dan. I think she should be extra nice to us," his friend chirps in.

I shove away from them, but his finger catches my fishnet tights, tearing a hole in them. I freeze, glancing down at the hole and then back at the guy.

"Oops," he says on a grin.

Anger rises hot and fast. "Did I give you permission to touch me?" I snap.

And then, as if to prove a point, he grabs my arse again. Without thought, I lash out, my fist colliding with his nose. Blood explodes, and he cries out, immediately releasing me.

"Argh! Fucking bitch."

Jackson, one of the security guys, sweeps in and pulls the guy to his feet, dragging him and his friend out of the club. I shake my hand because that bloody hurt.

"Are you okay, Delilah?" I turn to Stacey, one of the other girls. Concern mars her pretty face.

"I'm fine." Damn, my thumb is really throbbing.

Going down to the bar, I grab a towel and some ice, wrapping it around my hand. I disappear out back to the changing room and sit down for a moment. My thumb is already turning an ugly purple and swelling. There's a gaping hole in my fishnet tights too. I can just imagine Judas's reaction when I see him after work.

A few minutes later there's a knock on the door, and Stacey pops her head in. "Boss wants to see you, Delilah."

"He's here?"

She shrugs one shoulder. "Guess so." Shit. *Shit.*

Pushing to my feet, I follow her out; her long bleached blonde hair swaying with every step. She offers me a small, almost sympathetic smile before she goes back up the stairs to VIP, and I head for the stairs that lead to Judas's office. At the top, there's a door that opens onto a short corridor, and as soon as the door closes behind me, I can hear Judas shouting.

"What do I fucking pay you for if the girls have to defend themselves? What the fuck were you doing? You obviously weren't paying attention."

"I'm sorry, boss. It won't happen again."

"Get out."

The door in front of me opens, and I still like a rabbit in headlines as Jackson stands in front of me. All six and a half feet of him.

"Sorry, Lila," he says as he moves past me.

"It's fine. Don't apologise."

"Delilah, get in here," Judas barks.

On a deep breath, I walk into the office, closing the door behind me. I feel like a kid getting called to the principle's office, and the idea pisses me off.

Judas leans against the front of his desk, his head tilted down and his shoulders hunched forward. He says nothing for long moments, but his anger is like a living thing in the room with us. I refuse to fear him though.

Moving closer, I slide one leg between his spread ones, straddling his thigh. Cupping his face, I force him to look at me. The rage swirls in his irises, making the sharp angles of his face seem cold and hard.

"I handled it," I whisper, brushing my lips over his.

He grips my jaw, securing me in place. He holds me right in front of him, searching, probing. "He had your arse in his hand, Delilah. You should have hit him long before then." There's a chill in his voice that promises anarchy. That low menacing growl is like the prequel to his own personal apocalypse. This is the man that he really is, the one that I both fear and love.

"You saw?"

"I'm always watching you, little lamb." There was a time when that might have bothered me, but it doesn't. I love the way I'm the centre of his world. It's powerful and addictive, to be wanted like this. Maybe it's a little sick, but if that's the case, then I don't want to be cured.

I close my eyes, and his fingers dig into my cheeks harder. "Look, maybe you should stop coming to the club so much."

"You don't want me here?" There's a thinly veiled warning behind the question.

I open my eyes. "You were never here before. You're supposed to be lying low. I'm worried you'll do something to draw attention." Like kill someone for looking at me the wrong way. "This isn't like you. You aren't irrational."

His hand braces against the small of my back. "I am when it comes to you."

"You can't try and kill anyone who looks at me wrong."

He wrenches me up against him. "I can," he whispers in my ear. "Because you're mine."

"Always." I press a lingering kiss a to his lips for no other reason than I need it. I feel this connection between us growing stronger by the day, as though we're melding together. "But I don't want you to get in any trouble. I need you."

His eyes sweep over the tiny shorts and bralette that I'm wearing. "If you'd wear clothes—"

"We've talked about this."

"Then work in the office. Manage the books. I'll pay you the same."

I roll my eyes. "No, you won't because you pay me ten pounds an hour, and they," I point to the VIP area, "tip me hundreds a night."

"So I'll match it."

"No."

He grits his teeth, his fingers flinching against my hip. "Fuck, Delilah. What do you want me to do here?"

"Absolutely nothing."

"I swear you want me to go back to prison," he growls, sliding his hand over mine. Our fingers thread together, and he squeezes, making me wince. His brows furrow as he takes my hand, inspecting it. My thumb is swollen now, the skin so purple it's bordering on black. "You punched him?" I nod. "You kept your thumb inside your fist didn't you?"

"I don't know."

His eyes shift from my hand to my face. "What happened to eyes, throat, crotch?"

"I panicked."

"This is probably broken."

"Great. One more injury." His jaw works back and forth. "I'm fine."

He shakes his head. "Fucking Jackson standing there with his thumb up his arse."

"Poor guy is terrified of you."

"Good."

"So grumpy."

He cocks a brow. "I'm this close to firing you."

"What? Why? I didn't do anything."

"You know why." Because I won't just bow to him.

"You can't be this possessive. It's not normal."

"Oh, little lamb." He laughs, and then his teeth scrape over the side of my neck. "Nothing about us is normal."

His lips trail a path down to my shoulder, and my mind blanks, all thoughts just blinking out of existence. Grabbing a handful of his hair, I kiss him, a deep drugging kiss that turns my entire body limp.

His finger hooks into the top of my shorts. "Just let me pay you the money not to do the work."

I pull back. "Judas Kingsley, I will not be your whore!"

He smirks. "Of course not. I don't have to pay you to fuck you, sweet Delilah." He releases the button on my shorts and slowly lowers the zip.

"I'm working."

"I'm the boss."

He kisses his way down my neck again, pausing where it meets my shoulder and sinking his teeth into my skin. His fingers have just worked their way beneath the seam of my lace thong when there's a knock at the door. He shifts me until my back is fully to the door.

"Come in."

"Hey, there are police here." I recognise Marcus's thick cockney accent. Police? Oh god, they finally figured it out. They know I killed Isabelle. My heart ticks up a notch, and I imagine them dragging me through the nightclub in handcuffs, everyone looking, knowing what I did.

"I'll be there in a minute." Judas slips his hand from my underwear and zips and buttons my shorts. The door closes, and he pushes to his feet.

"Why are the police here?"

"I don't know."

"Judas…"

He clasps my face in both hands and kisses my forehead. "They aren't here for you, Delilah. Calm down." His fingers stroke over my face, his brows pulled tightly together. "Here." He hands me his keys. "Take my car. Go to my place. I'll be there soon."

Tipping my chin up, he kisses me quickly before striding from the room. *Stay calm.*

By the time Judas gets back, it's late, and my nerves are so fraught that I feel like I'm losing my mind.

"Well?"

He tosses his keys on the coffee table and shrugs out of his jacket. "They just wanted some CCTV footage from a fight we had last night."

I narrow my eyes, unsure whether to believe him. "I didn't see a fight."

"It was outside."

"Okay." But it's not okay. God, it's like I've immersed myself so entirely in Judas that I've forgotten why I ever went to him in the first place. Nothing has changed. I still helped kill Isabelle. Nate is still right there, lingering in the shadows, waiting. And his employers will still kill me if they think for a second that I'll talk. That impending sense of dread that has become blanketed under everything that is Judas rises now, wrapping its icy fingers around my throat.

A hand lands on my shoulder, and I jump, glancing at Judas.

"Delilah. It's okay." He says the words slowly like he's talking to a small child. "I need to take you to the hospital."

I shake my head, glancing at my hand wrapped in an ice pack. "It's fine."

Sitting next to me, he takes the pack and inspects my hand.

"I'm proud of you for throwing a punch, little lamb."

"I did it wrong."

"God loves a trier." That dashing smile crosses his lips, and I almost want to cry because I'm terrified that there will come a time when I'll never see his face again.

I rest my cheek on his shoulder, inhaling the clean citrus scent of him. "Let's just do normal for an hour or two."

He chuckles. "We're not normal, Delilah."

"Shh, just an hour."

And he gives it to me. His arms come around me, one hand stroking over my hair, and right here, right now, I feel like Judas would protect me from anything. But deep down I know he can't protect me from myself.

22

DELILAH

THERE'S a light knock on my bedroom door. I cross the room, pulling it open. Tiff stands there, her face pale and her eyes wide.

"Tiff, what's wrong?"

She sweeps her blonde hair behind her ear. "Lila, there are police here. They want to talk to you." I feel all the blood drain from my face and my pulse leaps into a sprint. A cold chill sweeps over my body and my palms grow clammy.

"Okay. Just...give me a second."

She nods and backs away from the door. Tiff's my friend, but I can see the suspicion on her face. She's wondering what I did. She's thinking that maybe she doesn't know me at all. And she'd be right.

I change into a pair of jeans and a hoody and leave the room. With each step down the stairs, my legs feel a little weaker, my lungs a little smaller. When I round the corner, I try and force myself to keep calm. Two police officers stand in my kitchen in full uniform.

"Hello," I say, my voice barely more than a squeak.

The pair of them round on me, and I shrink back. The

man is younger than the woman, and he offers me a small smile.

"Miss Thomas, we need to ask you some questions."

I nod. "Uh, yeah, sure. Can I...ask what this is about?"

The woman's expression is a hard mask. "Best that you come with us. We'll discuss it at the station."

The station? They want me to go to the station. My pulse throbs against my eardrums, drowning out everything else. "Am I in trouble?"

The guy takes a step forward. "We just need to ask some questions and for you to make a statement." He offers me a reassuring smile, but I don't feel reassured because I'm guilty. And aren't guilty people always found out in the end?

"Okay," I whisper.

When I get to the police station, I'm shown to a room and asked to wait. It's a plain room with a small table in it and two chairs facing each other. I'm so jittery that my hands are shaking, so I shove them into the pockets of my hoody and pace back and forth.

When the door finally clicks open, I'm ready to crawl out of my skin.

An older man with a kind smile and lines set into the corners of his eyes walks in. He has a paper folder tucked under his arm as he walks around the desk.

"Miss Thomas, I'm Detective Harford." He pulls out the chair and unfastens the button of his jacket before sitting. "Please sit."

I hesitate for a moment and then sit in the chair across from him. "I don't know why I'm here," I say.

His eyes meet mine, and though they're devoid of any kind of emotion, I feel like he's screaming at me that he knows what I did. "I just want to ask you some questions about the night of the twentieth of March." I say nothing, and he opens the file, sliding a piece of paper across the table to me. It's an image, a grainy CCTV snapshot of Charles and me. His arms are wrapped around my shoulders, and mine around his waist. A blinding smile covers his face, and we look like we could almost be lovers. "This image of you and Charles Stanley was taken that night." I swallow heavily and nod. "Can I ask how you know him?"

"He was my friend, Isabelle's boyfriend."

"Do you embrace all your friend's boyfriends like that?" He jerks his head toward the picture. I feel my face heat as he puts me on the spot.

"I...we were friends too."

The detective's lips press together tightly. He's not convinced. He takes another image from his file and slides that in front of me. Another CCTV image, this time of Nate and me. I'm pressed against him so tightly that I'm straddling one of his thighs and he's burying his face in my neck. "And this one? Was he a friend?"

My spine straightens at the bite in his voice. "No, Nate was my boyfriend."

"Was?"

"We're not together anymore." He leans back in his chair, propping one elbow on the back while his other hand raps over the tabletop. I'm going to go to prison, and then Nate's bosses are going to have me killed. I don't want to die. I don't want to go to jail.

Better. I need to be better. More convincing. "Look, I gave my statement about the night Isabelle and Charles died." My voice breaks. "What does this have to do with Nate?"

He takes another picture out of his file, then another, and another. All images of Nate with various people, giving them a half hug, slapping palms together, and one where they're just hunched close, obviously exchanging something, but the darkness of the image makes it hard to see clearly. "Your boyfriend is a drug dealer, Miss Thomas."

I look up at him, and for a moment I don't know what to say. I feel like he can see the truth written all over my face, he can read my lie. "He's not my boyfriend," I whisper.

His lips pull into a small smile that says he's got me and he knows it. "Interesting that of my statement, that's the bit you deny."

"I don't know anything about Nate dealing drugs," I say quickly.

"You don't seem surprised by it though. That would suggest you, in fact, did know."

I press my fingers to my temples and close my eyes for a second. I can't sell Nate out. "Look, Nate wasn't the nicest guy. I never asked how he made his money or what he did. Our relationship wasn't a long-term thing." I shrug one shoulder. "It wouldn't surprise me if he were, but I never saw anything."

He pushes the image of us together just an inch closer. "Not even when you were right there with him while he was working?"

"No." My voice quivers and my nerves are right there at breaking point.

"You know what I think, Miss Thomas?" I really don't want to know. He takes the image of Charles and me and lines it up next to the other picture. "I think this is you making a delivery." My heart trips over itself — falling flat before resuming a desperate, awkward splutter. "I don't think you know Charles Stanley well enough to hug him. This is just a drop." I hadn't realised I was chewing on my thumbnail until a sting of pain alerts me. Looking down, I see that my nail is now bleeding. His eyes follow mine, looking at the evidence of my obvious guilt. He leans forward over the desk, dropping his head to catch my gaze. "I don't know whether it was willing, or whether he forced you to do it." There's a pause, and his expression is now nothing but sympathetic. He's giving me an out, but I can't take it. "It's not you I'm after, Delilah. You're a student, a nice girl from a nice family. However, Nathaniel is a link in a chain much bigger. I want him so I can get to them." He opens his folder and takes out one final picture, placing it in front of me. I close my eyes, fighting back the sting of tears. I don't need to look at that picture because it's branded in my mind. The same image they splashed all over the main news channels. Isabelle's smiling face. "Your friend is dead, Delilah. Because of guys like him putting this stuff on the streets." Guys like Judas.

"I'm sorry," I choke. "I wish I could help you, but I don't know anything."

He blows out a long breath and scrubs a hand over his clean-shaven jaw. "We can protect you, Miss Thomas." They can't though. I've learned more in these past few months than I ever wanted to know about the criminal underbelly of London. I know how it works. These people make far too much money to ever let one girl pose a risk. The police can't protect me. No one can, except maybe Judas. "I'm giving you this chance. The next time we speak, I'll be arresting you for intent to supply and conspiracy. Not to mention aiding and abetting a murder." I swallow down the bile that's creeping up the back of my throat.

"I'm sorry. I really don't know anything." I know I sound hollow, my voice a hoarse croak. Truthfully, I'm terrified, but I probably should be. Even an innocent girl would be scared of those accusations, right? And I'm not innocent. I did exactly what he's saying I did.

Pushing to his feet, he shakes his head, and I hunch under the weight of his obvious disappointment. He thought I was a nice girl, a good person. He thought I would roll over on Nate, and I wish I could help him. I wish I was better, but I'm not. I'm looking out for myself.

"You're free to go." Scooping up all the pictures, he leaves the room.

By the time I've walked home from the police station, I'm in a full-scale panic. So much so that I don't notice the black BMW parked right outside my house until it's too late. The driver's door swings open and Nate gets out, straightening to his full height. I still, holding my hand up. It's broad daylight, but I don't trust him. As I look at him, all I see is the mad rage that painted his face that night, and all I feel is his hands at my throat, the blow to my face.

I slide my hand in my pocket, palming the knife that I always keep on me.

"What did you tell them?" he asks. How the hell does he know that I was with the police?

"Judas is on his way here," I lie. "You should leave."

"What. Did. You. Tell. Them?" he growls, edging closer.

"Touch me, and I'll scream," I warn. His nostrils flare, his fists clenching at his sides. He's not going anywhere. "I told them I didn't know anything, okay? You were right. They wanted me to flip on you. I told them I couldn't help them. Now leave."

He visibly relaxes, though his eyes narrow in suspicion. "Why would you do that, hey?"

"Because I don't want to die! I don't want any of this."

Nate laughs. "Don't want it? You're fucking Judas Kingsley." He pushes off the car and comes closer. I back away again. "You think I'm bad? You have no idea the things the Kingsley brothers have done."

"I know what he does," I say, my voice gaining strength.

He smirks. "Do you? He's fucking with you, Lila. Playing you. What interest could a guy like that possibly have with a girl like you?"

"Nate, just leave."

"Of course you could turn it around, use him, play him…"

I frown and rub my throbbing temples. "What?"

"I still love you, Lila. We could—"

My high-pitched laugh cuts through the air. "Oh my god. You beat me up, Nate! You're a fucking psycho!"

He creeps closer again, and again, I back up. "I was just so mad when I thought you were working for him." His jaw tenses. "I didn't think you were fucking him," he spits. And if he had, I'm sure he probably would have killed me, even though I wasn't sleeping with Judas at the time.

"So you think I'm going to leave Judas and come running back to you?" Has he always been this crazy? Did I just not see it?

"Is it the money, Lila? The nightclubs and the fast cars? Thought you'd move up in the world?"

"Fuck you, Nate," I snap, growing braver. "He's helping me. I have a job that doesn't involve—"

"Ah, yes, in Fire. The very place that you helped to shut down." He smirks. "That golden pussy must be working a treat for him to overlook that." He eyes me up and down. "But it's all fixed now, right? A couple of dead kids aren't enough to keep a Kingsley down." There's something about the way he says it, the maniacal look in his eyes, the twisted grin on his lips.

I decide to edge around the other side of his car, and he smirks as he watches me move, delighting in the fact that I'm scared of him. I reach in my pocket, readying my keys as

I shove through my front gate and dash towards the door. My heart hammers and my hands shake, but I manage to get the door open. Stepping inside, I close the door on the image of Nate standing just the other side of the gate.

"Keep your mouth shut, Lila," he says before it slams.

Closing my eyes, I release the breath that has my lungs screaming.

"Lila?"

Lifting my head, I find Tiff standing in the hallway, her fingers knotting in the bottom of her over-sized t-shirt.

"Don't worry, Tiff, it's fine."

She nods but chews her bottom lip. "Look, if you need a solicitor, my family has a really good one."

I smile. "That's kind. Thank you. But it's fine. It was just a mix-up."

She frowns. "Lila, you've been at the station for over two hours. You don't have to lie to me."

On a sigh, I give her a variation of the truth. "They know that Nate deals," I say. It's not new information to her. Most party people around campus know that Nate deals, just not that I helped him. "They thought that I was still his girl-friend, and now they want me to flip on him."

She shakes her head, her blonde hair falling around her face. "What did you tell them?"

I shrug one shoulder. "That I didn't know anything."

"But, everyone knows that Nate deals..."

"I want nothing to do with any of it, Tiff."

"But you know he probably gave Izzy those drugs..."

I pinch the bridge of my nose. "What do you think he'll do to me if I talk?" I lower my hand, and our eyes meet. "He's a drug dealer, Tiff. He's not a good guy."

Her face crumples, sympathy crossing over her features. "You do know how to pick them."

I roll my eyes. "Thanks."

"At least Judas seems nice." She smiles. "I mean, he's a priest. You couldn't really get any more different." Of course, you meet a guy one time, wearing a dog collar and he must be golden.

A small laugh slips from my lips. "Yep. He's a keeper." Shoving away from the door, I move past her.

"Well, you know where I am if you need me," she calls after me.

"Thanks." Tiff is a nice girl. I guess at one point I was a nice girl, or at least I tried to be, but now I can barely remember that time. Honestly, I think I've always been a little tainted, and with each terrible bad-boy boyfriend, I got progressively worse. Until Nate. I never even knew how bad he was until I was a few months in, and by that point, Nate had become like a drug of sorts. A progressive rush. Each step I took with him was like moving onto something harder until I was finally at that destructive point of no return. Rock bottom. Dealing drugs, living for the rush, secretly hoping that maybe, just maybe I'd get caught. Picturing the look on my father's face when he realised just how far his perfect daughter had fallen. There was a certain satisfaction in it.

I chose Nate because he was bad. And then there's Judas, who was never a choice. He found me at rock bottom and instead of picking me up, he whispered for me to delve a little deeper, to embrace the squalor of my damned soul.

I'm no longer the naïve girl wrapped up in her guilt, but I'd be lying if I said I wasn't scared. I've only just found myself. I don't want to lose it all.

Collapsing on my bed, I let out a long breath and close my eyes, trying to block everything out.

My phone buzzes, and I glance at the screen, seeing a

text from Judas. Just the thought of him chases the panic away a little, and I pick up my phone, reading the message.

Judas: I've been having carnal thoughts about you all day.

I smile and type out a response.

Me: I miss you, too.

Judas: Are you okay?

I start typing out a response, then stop. Then start again. On the fourth time of me deleting the message, attempting to construct a cheerful lie, my phone rings. His name flashes across the screen, and I answer it.

"Hey."

"What's wrong?" he asks, and I can picture the way his brows will be pulled tightly together, the small line in his forehead marring the perfect, ethereal planes of his face.

"Nothing." I rub a hand over my face. I don't want to see him because I need to stand alone on this, but then the thought hits me: I might go to prison. There's nothing like an impending axe hanging over your head to make you feel like life is short. "Where are you?"

"At the church."

"I'll come and see you." I hang up the phone before he can answer.

The walk over to the church isn't as quiet as usual. It's the middle of the afternoon and London is buzzing with its usual obnoxious traffic. People hurry past me, walking to their next meeting, or rushing to get home early.

As I cross the park, I see the teenagers playing football, shouting loudly and heckling each other, skidding on the grass in their school uniforms. And yet, when I reach the church and cross the threshold, the same calming peace washes over me. It never changes. Sometimes there may be worshippers in here, people praying and lighting candles.

Other times I can be utterly alone, but it's always serene. Silent.

Today, no one is here, but I know that Judas will be in the confessional. The curtain on the other side is open. With muted steps, I approach the booth and tug the curtain closed, before going to the side the priest sits in. I expect to find him sitting there, but instead, he's standing, his back braced to the partition and a sexy smile pulling at his lips.

"Really?" he says.

"Really." Stepping inside, I tug the curtain closed. Instantly, the air in the confined space becomes thick. Reaching out, he trails one finger over the side of my neck and down my chest to the top of my cleavage.

I close the distance between us, pushing up on my tiptoes to place my lips to his. This right here is my peace. He's like coming home. His fingers wind around my waist, and he lifts me off my feet, turning us so he can slam me up against the partition. The entire confessional trembles under the force of it, and I squeeze my thighs around his hips.

"Did you come to confess, sweet Delilah?" he breathes against my mouth.

"I came to rid you of those carnal thoughts," I gasp, my breaths coming in short, sharp gasps.

"Hmm. Well, you aren't helping."

My fingers slide into his hair, tugging him closer to my throat. "I'm turning thought into reality."

The heat of his palms meets the back of my thighs, sliding up until he's cupping my arse in both hands. "You going to fuck me in the confessional, little lamb?" he asks, nipping just below my ear.

"I am but your humble servant."

"Such a filthy little sinner."

Dropping me to my feet, he shoves the skirt of my dress up and hooks his fingers into the lace of my underwear. Gathering the material at my hips, he yanks, shredding them. Excitement races through my veins, and the anticipation has my heart thrumming like a stampede of wild horses. Here, in this place, this feels so wrong, and I love it. I fumble for his belt, yanking the leather open and reaching for the button on his trousers. Fingers wind through my hair again, but this time he uses his grip to turn me around, shoving my chest up against the divider. Oh god, if anyone walks into the other side of the confessional, they'll know exactly what we're doing. It shouldn't turn me on this much, but I think I love the idea of desecrating sacred ground every bit as much as I love Judas defiling me. I want a witness to our depravity. Two bad souls who shouldn't be in the house of the Lord, soiling it. Judas kicks my legs apart and trails his fingers up the inside of my thigh. I can hardly breathe by the time he reaches the top.

"Judas," I beg. A small laugh slips from him, and he places a feather-light kiss to the nape of my neck.

"Patience." Then he slams two fingers inside me so hard that I'm forced onto my tiptoes inside my boots. My palm smacks against the partition, seeking some kind of grip. He groans against my ear, and I twist my head against his brutal hold of my hair, his lips slam over mine, and I swallow the feral sound. "So fucking wet, Delilah," he hisses against my lips, pushing into me even harder.

One second I'm against the wall with the full weight of Judas at my back, the next he's gone, but he wrenches me back by my hair. I take steps backwards until my legs bump against his knees, and I realise that he's sitting on the pew.

He forces me to straddle his thighs, my back to his chest.

Oh god, we're really doing this. He's going to fuck me in a confessional.

He softens his grip on my hair and guides me over him. "Judas," I moan because he feels so good, so right — so wrong.

He thumps his head back against the wood behind him and a low groan slips from his lips. "Fuck, Delilah."

He releases his hold and moves both hands to my hips. He doesn't lift me, simply rolls my body over him, and it's like he's pumping pure electricity over every inch of my skin. My spine bows, my head goes back, and a string of noises slip from my lips. He wraps a hand around my mouth and plasters me to his chest.

"Quiet," he breathes against my ear.

It's dirty and sordid, sinful in every way, and I want it. I'd say a thousand Hail Mary's for this, for him. He makes me feel owned and yet cherished, tarnished and yet born anew. In his arms, I'm lost and found all at once. The pieces of me that were once broken are now simply his.

Everything builds within me like this pressure just begging to be released. Judas manipulates every movement until I'm desperate for something only he can give me.

He holds me on a cliff edge for what feels like forever, and then his grip on my hip tightens until he's buried inside me so deep that I'm not sure where he ends and I begin. And I want it. I want him in me, a part of me. I want the lines to blur so much that we're one and the same: the priest and his worshipper. I want to pray at his fucked up altar.

I fall apart, muscles tensing as pleasure rips through them. Stars dot my vision, and my head spins. I cry out, into the palm of Judas's hand, and he holds me through it, letting me ride it out.

"Fuck, Delilah." Releasing my mouth, he shoves me

forward roughly, using me like his own personal doll. All I can hear is his laboured breaths, my racing pulse, and the creaking of old wood that's never played witness to this kind of abuse.

"Fuck!" Judas's movements become stiff and jilted before he stills, a guttural growl tearing from him.

For a moment neither of us moves. My head hangs forward spilling long hair between Judas's parted knees in front of me. His palms smooth over my arse and down my thighs. Our too-loud breaths blend, sounding like the epicentre of a thunderstorm in the quiet of the church. If anyone is here, there's no way they didn't hear that.

When my legs have stopped trembling, I stand and bend down, grabbing my handbag. I take a tissue out, but Judas pushes to his feet and steals it from me. Nudging me back against the partition again, he kisses me long and slow, his hand dipping between my legs and wiping his come from the inside of my thighs. My cheeks heat, but my heart skips happily at the tenderness of the gesture. Then he pulls away and hands the tissue back to me.

"What am I supposed to do with that?"

He smirks. "Keepsake?"

"You're gross."

He laughs and kisses me once more before fastening his trousers and yanking back the confessional curtain. I press myself back against the pew, trying to hide, just in case there's someone out there. "Come on," he says, offering me his hand. I toss the tissue under the pew, smirking to myself because I'm pretty sure he'll have to clean that up later. The great Judas Kingsley, hot, richer-than-sin crime lord, picking up grotty come-covered tissues from the confessional.

. . .

Judas leads me back to the office, and I hop up on his desk, waiting while he puts some cash in the safe.

"You haven't told me what's wrong," he says.

"Because I had so much chance?"

Cocking a brow, he tugs at the dog collar at his throat. "I believe it was you who accosted me in the confessional." His lips quirk. "So determined to sin, Delilah."

I duck my head. "I got arrested."

I feel the change in the air. Flirty and fun Judas disappears, and without even looking, I know I now have bad Judas. The guy who has the ability to scare me, even though I know he would never hurt me.

"What?" His voice is like ice being scraped from a windscreen on a January morning.

I lift my gaze. "They know."

"And you didn't think to tell me this on the phone? You thought we should fuck first?"

"Fuck you, Judas!"

"Do they have proof? No, you'd still be there if they did," he muses, answering his own question.

"He wanted me to flip on Nate."

"What did you say?"

"That I don't know anything. I'm not stupid! I know his bosses will come after me. But Nate knows they questioned me." Oh god, now he looks mad.

"He called you?" I can hear the barely restrained fury, and I shift on the desk, wishing I could back up without drawing attention to the movement.

"He came to my house." He turns away from me, and I watch the muscles in his back roll and flex through the material of his shirt. "I think he was just driving his threat home."

"The boy has very little regard for his life."

"He said something…"

"What?" He twists his head towards me.

"Nate's mad that we're together. He was trying to get to me, and he said, 'I guess it takes more than a couple of dead kids to keep a Kingsley down'." I shake my head, watching his eyes narrow. "It could be nothing, but the way he said it… It was like he was annoyed that Fire was open again. But he deals at Fire. It was his main source of business before it closed. Why would he want it to stay closed?"

"Did he touch you?" I shake my head, and he comes closer, his eyes searching mine.

"Nate isn't the problem right now." I release a long breath and fall forward, resting my forehead to his chest. His hands smooth down my back, stroking the length of my hair. "What am I going to do, Judas?" I slide my palm up his chest, feeling the steady beat of his heart. "I don't want to leave you." My voice cracks and my eyes prickle with tears. His chin rests on top of my head — his hot breath stirring the strands of my hair.

"I won't let anything happen to you, Delilah."

I sniff back tears and scrunch a handful of his shirt. "You can't promise that, Judas. I'm guilty." I shake my head and lift my face from his chest. He glances down at me, a small smirk playing over his lips.

"Little lamb, you forget who I am." He presses his lips to mine. "I'm a Kingsley. We run this city."

And as he speaks the words, I believe him, the same way I always believe Judas. I trust him when he says he'll protect me, and I never feel safer than when I'm right here, in his arms.

Judas is a bad man, and it's that which keeps me safe. The devil protects his own.

23

JUDAS

I LIE THERE, listening to Delilah's soft breaths. My bedroom that once smelled of cologne and laundry detergent is now laced with the sweet vanilla scent that seems to cling to her skin. I slowly pull my arm away from her, my fingertips brushing over the satin-soft skin of her waist. She stirs, a soft sigh leaving her lips before she settles back against the pillows once more.

Slipping from the bed, I leave the room, pulling the door closed with a hushed click. The apartment is dark and silent — the only sound the incessant ticking of the clock on the living room wall. Somewhere beyond the walls, a cat starts yowling, and there's the distant wail of an ambulance siren.

Taking a seat at the dining room table, I scroll through my phone until I land on Jase's number. Tapping it, I listen to the dial tone.

"Judas, how are you?"

"I need you to look into something for me."

"Great. Yeah, I'm good, thanks," Jase mutters sarcastically.

"Jase," I growl.

He huffs out a breath. "Fuck me, you're almost as bad as Saint."

"That's a bit extreme."

He laughs. "What do you need?"

"Could you hunt down an autopsy report?"

He sucks on his teeth. "Tricky, but it can be done. Give me a couple of days. Whose report?"

"Isabelle Wright."

"Done. As it's you, and we're family, I'll charge you the usual." He laughs again and hangs up. The family thing is a running joke to Jase. If Saint didn't pay him so well, I'm sure his loyalty would fall elsewhere.

And thinking of Saint...he's next.

I dial again, and I'd be lying if I said my heart rate doesn't rise a little as I wait to hear my brother's voice. He has this way of making the most hardened men nervous. My father doesn't even like being in a room with him.

"Judas."

"Saint."

"What do you want?"

"We need to meet." What I have to discuss with him, he definitely won't want to talk about over the phone. You could be on an encrypted line, and the paranoid fucker would still shit a brick.

"Fine. Your church, tomorrow morning."

"What? You never do morning meetings."

"Do you want an appointment or not?"

I sigh. "Fine. What time?"

"Nine." The lines goes dead, and I frown. Does he ever sleep?

The corner lamp suddenly comes on, and I squint against the light spilling into the room. Delilah leans against the wall right next to it, an over-sized jumper hanging from one shoulder, the ends of the sleeves scrunched in her balled fists. She hugs herself, and the material rides up, revealing her lace underwear beneath. Those damn woolly socks are pulled up, one over her knee and the other slipping below. She's the picture of innocence, and it makes me want to bury my dick in her and dirty her up. Every fucking time.

"What are you doing?" she asks, her voice still raspy with sleep.

"Come here."

She obeys immediately, walking over to where I sit in the shadows. My fingers trail over the soft skin at the back of her thigh, and I tug her forward until she folds into my lap, her legs spread either side. I slide my palms under her jumper, feeling the searing heat of her back. Curling into a ball, she presses herself to my chest, tucking her head beneath my chin. She's like a warm, sleepy little kitten.

"Why are you up?" she whispers.

"I had to make some calls."

"You know, you can do your whole bad guy thing in front of me," she mumbles, and I laugh.

"Bad guy thing?"

She nods against my throat. "You don't have to sneak out of bed."

"There was no sneaking."

She lifts her head and drapes her arms over my shoulders. Full lips tilt in a playful smile as her eyes drop to my mouth. "Well, if that were true, then I'd still be in bed with the hot priest." Leaning in, she brushes her lips over the corner of my mouth. "Instead, I'm out here with this dodgy-looking drug boss."

"So you think the priest is hotter?"

She shrugs her bare shoulder, and her arms tighten,

folding around my neck. "Oh, I don't know. I've always had a thing for bad boys."

"That so?" Grabbing her arse, I stand up, placing her back down on the dining room table.

"Mmmhmm." She brings her lips to my ear. "That's why I fucked the priest in a confessional. Then he was so very bad."

I groan, and she sits back, looking up at me through those long lashes. One side of her bottom lip disappears between her teeth, and she has no idea what that look does to me. The girl can turn my dick to stone with a glance.

Placing my lips to her neck, I swipe my tongue over her skin. My fingers meet the lace of her underwear and the breathy little gasp that leaves her is the sweetest sound. Pushing the lace to the side, I ram two fingers inside her, and it's beautiful, it really is. Her lips part, her lashes sweeping over her cheekbones as waves of dark hair tumble to her waist. Everything pauses for a second, the world holding its breath to witness her perfection.

Her nails rake over the back of my neck, and I smile as she starts to lose control. She's so responsive, so compliant, so wet for me.

"I want to taste you, little lamb," I breathe against the length of her exposed throat.

Dropping to my knees, I wrench her underwear to the side and do exactly that. She tastes like sin and salvation, sweet temptation and burning torture. Her hand goes to my hair, nails scratching over my scalp.

"Judas." Her voice trembles along with her thighs, her entire body pulled tight like the string of a bow, just waiting to release. Her back hits the dining room table, and her legs drape over my shoulders. The way her body contorts, it's like she's possessed, and I'm an exorcist trying to tear her in half.

Within seconds, she lets it fly, fracturing apart as she does. With every touch, every caress of my tongue over her body, each movement of my fingers, she comes to life. When her body finally relaxes, she crumples like a broken little doll.

Pushing to my feet, I look down at her sprawled on my dining room table, her dark hair spilling around her as her chest rises and falls heavily.

"If you think you can distract me, it won't work," she pants.

I laugh, pushing her jumper up and kissing her stomach. "Ah, sweet Delilah, I have you right where I want you. And you're completely distracted."

Sitting up, she slides from the table and simply walks across the living room, her hips swinging. "Are you coming to bed?" She flashes me a sensuous smile, and I find myself following her instinctually. Now who's distracted?

I spot Saint sitting in the front pew, his head dropped to his chest and his hands clasped in front of him. Even from here, there's something about Saint that's just fundamentally wrong. He's too still. Like when you walk into woodland and hear no bird call; it's unsettling. Unnatural. That is what Saint is; the stone cold silence of a forest with a predator in its midst. I take a seat beside him and wait because I know what he's like about communing with God. After a few moments, he lifts his head and stares straight ahead.

"You wanted to talk, so talk."

"I need a favour."

He finally turns his gaze to me, ice-cold eyes searching for weaknesses. "Your favours are growing tiresome, Judas."

I sigh. He's so dramatic. "Two in the last couple of months. Before that, the last time I asked you for anything we were fourteen, and I had to owe you a sin just so you wouldn't run your mouth to Ma."

"I don't hand out favours."

"Then I'll owe you."

"You can't owe more than one sin at a time." We put these rules in place when we were twelve after I owed Saint so many sins that he decided to cash in all on one day. We went to a strict Catholic school, and we were constantly trying to get the other expelled. He made me slash the head teacher's tyres, start a fire in the cafeteria, punch David Loughton in the nose and get caught finger-fucking Daisy Johnson in the girl's locker room. That last one got me expelled.

"We aren't twelve anymore."

"The rules are the rules." He lifts a brow. "Tell me what you want, and I'll consider."

"You have half the police in London on your payroll. I need you to find out what they have in relation to the Isabelle Wright case."

"Ah, yes, the girl who overdosed in your club. Careless, Judas."

"There's a girl they're looking into. She's linked to Nathaniel Hewitt. I think he works for the Moretti family."

"What's her name?"

"Delilah Thomas."

He says nothing for long moments. "You want to know what they have on her."

"I need her. Not behind bars."

"Why? What is she to you?" His eyes narrow. I can't tell him about Delilah. Saint loves nothing more than a weakness, and by giving him this; I'm basically showing him my throat.

"I suspect that there is more to this overdose. I have a plan to fuck over the Italians. I just need her in order to pull it off ..." He says nothing, simply staring, waiting. I roll my eyes. "She knows a lot about the Moretti's operation."

"And yours?"

I know where he's going with this. The idea that Delilah might know something will be enough to set Saint on edge. One wrong word to the police and they have a warrant to go through everything. He and I are linked by more than just blood thanks to Harold Dawson.

"She doesn't know anything about my business."

He stares at me until it becomes uncomfortable, but I'm used to it with Saint. I know not to show him that it unsettles me. "Is she business or pleasure?"

"Business," I say instantly because if he thinks she's anything more, he'll use her to fuck with me. Such is the way Saint thinks and operates.

A slow smile pulls at his lips, and I know from that one look that I've made an error. "I'll find out what you want, and I'll put a stop to any investigation into the girl, but you'll owe me a sin."

"You just said I couldn't owe you more than one."

"I'm cashing one in."

My chest tightens in anticipation because I just know he's about to drop a bomb. "What do you want me to do?"

His eyes lock with mine, nothing but pure calculation shining through them. "Kill Delilah Thomas."

My fists clench, and my heart stumbles for a beat, but I keep it all off my face. "Why?"

"She's either a weakness or a liability. Either way,

brother, you're coming to me, asking me to help this girl. The very fact that she needs help makes her a problem."

"I told you I need her. She's just a girl."

He pushes to his feet and smooths a hand down the front of his jacket. "Then she should be no great loss. Get what you need and kill her."

Fuck. Fuck! "I'm not going to kill her, Saint." He pauses halfway up the aisle and turns to face me.

"Oh? So she is pleasure then?" He's pleased with himself, delighted in fact. He's got me right where he wants me, and what can I do? Right now? Nothing.

"She's useful." I'm lying through my teeth, and I know he sees it.

He smirks and turns away, strolling towards the doors. "What was it father always said? Everyone but family is disposable."

"I'll need time," I shout after him.

"A week should be sufficient," he calls without ever turning around. God, he's a dick.

24

DELILAH

When I get out of class, I head across campus and start walking to the tube station. A car rolls to a halt beside me and the window rolls down.

"Get in," a familiar voice calls. Judas.

I open the door and slide into the leather seat. "Did I forget we were supposed to meet or something?"

His face looks as though it's carved from granite as he pulls back out into the stream of traffic. "We need to talk."

"That doesn't sound good." Judas has been distant for the last few days, constantly busy. I haven't even stayed at his place for the past two nights. Nate said he would tire of me. Does he know something I don't?

His hand lands on my thigh, and it's really doing nothing to reassure me. We drive for a few minutes, and then he pulls into a car park in front of a small park. The engine cuts and the following silence feels oppressive in the space of the car.

"Look, if you're not happy..."

He frowns at me. "Delilah. Don't be ridiculous." His fingers grip the steering wheel tightly as he stares through the windscreen at a couple of kids kicking a football around.

"What's going on?" I whisper.

"You didn't kill Isabelle and Charles."

"What?"

"Their tox reports had been buried, but after you told me what Nathaniel said, 'a couple of dead kids isn't enough to keep a Kingsley down', I had someone look into it." I swallow around the sudden lump in my throat and swipe my clammy palms over my skirt. "They found MDMA and PMA in their blood. In high doses."

"The pills were bad?"

His gaze meets mine. "A trace of PMA in a pill could be a mistake, a bad pill, but this is not a mistake."

"So the pills Nate gave me were deliberately laced to kill?"

"Yes, but they could have got them from somewhere else after you saw them. Or..."

"Or what?"

"Or Nate created a couple of dead kids to try and keep a Kingsley down."

I pull my knees to my chest and rest my forehead on them. This is not happening. "He wouldn't kill someone," I say, but hysteria is already creeping in.

"The same way he wouldn't beat his girlfriend to a pulp?"

"Oh my god." I close my eyes as my thoughts start buzzing through my head like swarming bees. "That's fucked up, Judas. What do we do? I have to tell the police."

"Delilah." He waits until I turn my head to the side and meet his gaze. "You need proof. At this stage, if we turn this over to them, all it proves is that her death was very much intentional and not an accident. The big red arrow still points to you. You're the only person that they can remotely say had contact with Isabelle or her boyfriend."

"Shit." I drag a trembling hand through my hair. "He framed me."

He looks back out the windscreen. "You're his scapegoat. He threatens you, so he knows you'll keep quiet. The police will get what they need, and send you down for his crime."

I swipe angrily at the tears that trickle down my cheeks. I'm mad. I'm mad at Nate for being such a dick, for making me believe that he cared for me when I was nothing more than a naïve pawn. I'm mad for Isabelle because everyone is out there thinking she's just a stupid girl who took one too many pills and killed herself. In reality, she was just a girl out for a good time. I'm angry at the injustice of it all — at the fact that Nate will probably get away with it.

"We need more than just that tox report." He regards me for a moment. "We're going to give them what they want."

"And what is that?"

"You're going to give the police what they want. You're going to hand them Nate."

"Are you insane? They'll kill me."

"No." He tucks a stray strand of hair behind my ear. "They won't. I have a plan."

My chest constricts, and suddenly the air in the car feels thin. Throwing the door open, I step outside and walk a little way into the park. I hear a car door slam behind me.

"Delilah!"

I still, tipping my head back and sucking in deep lungfuls of air. I sense Judas right behind me, but he doesn't touch me. "Why are you doing this?" I turn and face him. He stands with his hands in the pockets of his suit trousers. I want to believe that he would do this for me, but everything I know of men like Judas Kingsley tells me not to be so damn naïve — like I was with Nate. If I do this...I'd be trusting him with my life. "You want to get back at Nate for fucking you over?"

"Is that what you think?"

"I think you're a businessman."

Stepping forward, he wraps a hand around the back of my neck, tugging me until I'm plastered against him. The warm spring breeze whips around us, sending my hair sprawling across my face.

I clutch his wrist, and his forehead touches mine. An unspoken answer. "This can't be business, Judas."

"You're so far from business, little lamb." His voice is clipped and strained.

God, I'm in so much trouble with him. He holds my heart in his hand, and he doesn't even know. I wonder when Judas became so vital to me. When did he become the centre of my world?

"I hate this," I breathe.

"Look at me." I meet the deep blue of his gaze, but for once, there's no mischievous glint, no hardened façade, just...him. And I don't think I ever realised how guarded he usually is until this point. I feel like I can see his soul, his truth. "I'm walking a fine line here, Delilah. It's in my nature to destroy anything that gets in my way. Nathaniel normally wouldn't be a blip on my radar, but now your fate is entwined with his. He's holding a gun to your head, and in turn mine."

I swallow the lump in my throat. My problems have become his, and I never wanted that. "I know." I stroke over his jaw. "I'm sorry."

"Don't be. Just trust me?"

"Okay. What do you need me to do?"

"Get in the car. We're going to the police station."

A knot forms in the pit of my stomach. I trust him. He won't let anything happen.

———

Detective Harford walks around the corner, a smile breaking across his face when he sees me.

"Miss Thomas. What can I do for you?"

I inhale a deep breath. "I'll tell you what you need to know about Nathaniel Hewitt. But I want full immunity. I want to walk out of here today, and I want your assurance that Nate will never know that it was me."

He narrows his eyes and nods once. "I can do that."

I spend three hours in one room answering endless questions. How long did I sell for Nate? How much did I see? Did I see any of his associates? Had I overheard any phone calls? I tell them everything I know, and add a little bomb courtesy of Judas. He assures me it will blow up and from the look on the detectives face when I said those six words — he works for the Moretti family — I'd say he's right.

By the time I get out of there I'm tired, grumpy, and hungry.

Judas sends me a text: *I'm outside.*

His car lingers at the kerb, and when I get in, he hands me a paper bag. Opening it, I see a sub sandwich inside, turkey and ham. My favourite.

"Thanks."

He pulls away from the curb. "How did it go?"

I shrug. "I've given them what they need, and I'm not locked up for intent to supply."

He smiles and places his hand on my thigh. "Good. This will work. I promise."

For once, I hope I haven't placed faith the wrong guy. Honestly though, at this point, if Judas were to betray me, I think I'd rather die than live through the aftermath. Such is the lengths to which I've fallen under his spell. He feels like my reason for existing now.

25

JUDAS

IT WORKED PERFECTLY. The lead detective received the toxi-cology report and arrested Nathaniel within hours of Delilah making her statement. Of course, I want more time, but I've run out of choices. I have Saint breathing down my neck with a ticking clock, and Delilah is in several sets of crosshairs. I thought I would have time to watch my little sinner grow, to nurture her, but the time is up. It's now or never. Do or die. She'll either succeed or she'll fail.

I pull up in the multi-storey car park and stop beneath the flickering orange glow of one of the overhead lights. There's an eerie silence that puts me on edge, and I jump when the car door opens.

Tommy Ingleston slips into the passenger seat and glances at me. He's young and severe, his sharp black suit perfectly tailored and his dark hair combed into place. A pair of glasses covers the permanent scowl on his features.

"Tommy."

He nods. "Judas." His father worked for my Dad and uncle. Best solicitor in the country, my Dad used to say. The man kept *them* out of jail, so he couldn't be much short of a miracle worker.

I pull away and make the short drive across the city to Scotland Yard. Pulling into a taxi rank, I turn to him.

"I doubt he has representation yet, but if he does, you simply tell them you were sent by a mutual friend. He'll assume it's the Moretti's. Fabricate evidence if you have to. He needs to roll over on them. Be sure to remind him what the penalty is for double homicide."

He nods his head and gets out of the car without a word. Tommy is strange, but he's damn good at what he does. Takes after his father.

I sit there and wait. Minutes turn to hours, and I sigh, cracking my back as stiffness sets in. The traffic thins out until only a few cars splutter by now and then. My phone rings, and I glance at the screen, seeing Delilah's name.

"Little lamb."

"Judas, where are you?"

"Handling some business."

There's a sigh. "I don't like being here. What if they know where I live?"

"Delilah, calm down. The Moretti's won't even know that Nathaniel has been arrested yet. You're safer there with your friends than alone." I hate this; that I'm doing this to her, but I have to. She needs what is about to come every bit as much as I do. I can fix all of this, but I need her to evolve. "Just stay where you are. I'll see you later." I hang up the phone, gripping it tightly in my hand. This is my path. This is God's will, his test. We have to pass it.

Hours later and Tommy finally walks out the front of the building. Crossing the road, he gets in my car.

"Well?"

He smooths a hand over his tie. "He's going to inform on

his employers in exchange for his freedom. He'll have a few hours on bail to organise his affairs, and then he'll go into witness protection."

"How long until he's released?"

He checks his watch. "Within a couple of hours. They'll be watching him."

"And he knows the evidence against him?" He nods. "Perfect." Reaching into the centre console, I pull out an envelope of cash, handing it to him. "Thank you for your services."

Another jerky nod and he gets out of the car. I watch in the rearview mirror as he disappears into the night like a shadow that never was.

I sit and wait, long into the night, until finally, Nathaniel staggers from the front of the building. For a moment, he just stands there, as I guess I might if my entire life had been destroyed. Until I went after the person I thought was responsible — in this case, the one person whose 'evidence' had forced me into that shitty corner.

Turning, he starts walking with purpose. He hails a cab a little way down the street, and I pull out, following it. Sure enough, he goes straight to Delilah's house. My heart starts beating frantically in my chest, and I will it to calm as I pull up on the other side of the street and cut the engine. He gets out of the cab, and I wait, wondering if Myrina actually came through on delaying his tail. Five minutes, that's all I need.

Nathaniel steps up to the front door and looks both ways up and down the street. All the lights in the house are off, which means everyone must be asleep. Taking my phone out, I pull up Delilah's number, my finger lingering over the call button. She can't be asleep. I assume Nathaniel will pick the lock or know where a spare key is, but instead, he uses his elbow to smash one of the glass panels. There's no way anyone in the house wouldn't hear that. So I drop my phone and watch.

What's his plan here? Kill all four girls in the house? Excitement rushes through my veins. This is it, the moment where Delilah will descend into the smouldering pits of darkness, where she will bathe in blood and depravity. Or... she'll die, and we were never meant to be. *Now sin for me, little lamb. Prove you are worthy.*

26

DELILAH

I JERK AWAKE AT A SOUND. Sitting bolt upright, I strain to hear over my hammering heart. Nothing. Glancing at the alarm clock, I see it's two in the morning. I've still not heard anything from Judas. What if something's happened to him? What if the Moretti's found out what we did?

I still when I hear a creak from the stairs. Holding my breath, I listen intently. There's another creak, and I know it's the floorboard two steps away from my door. It's probably just Summer. She gets up in the night. There's the ominous slow squeak of my doorknob turning, and I freeze as though my lack of movement will make me invisible. When the door drifts open, I can just about make out the hulking shadowy form in my doorway. Adrenaline floods my veins, and I leap off the bed and dive towards the window. I don't know where I'm going, but I'm like a fleeing animal just looking for a way out.

Something tangles in my hair, and I'm wrenched back against a hard body. "I warned you, Lila." Nate. His hand goes to my throat, and hot breath assaults my neck, forcing bile up from my stomach. For a few seconds, all I do is panic, my limbs flailing frantically. *He's going to kill me. He's going to kill me!* "Scream, and I'll snap your pretty fucking neck."

Turning, he throws me on the bed, the full weight of his body landing on top of me. Fingers resume their hold on my throat, squeezing.

"I was just going to kill you, but I think you owe me, seeing as you ruined my fucking life," he hisses. His free hand trails up my thigh, and I whimper, turning my head to the side and squeezing my eyes closed. "You going to give it up to me one last time, Lila? Or shall I just take it." He laughs, his breath washing over my cheek. I count to ten in my head, trying to remain calm. *Just wait.* Opening my eyes, I focus on the bedside table, on the dim red light of the alarm clock.

Nate pushes himself off me, reaching for his belt, and it's in that tiny moment that I manage to shift my weight and lunge for the bedside table. My fingers wrap around the wooden hilt of the knife, and I wince as I contort my injured thumb to flick the blade out. Nate's full weight falls on me again, and he tries to grapple with me in the darkness. I start swinging wildly, panic driving me to just do something.

"Fuck." He pulls back slightly, but not enough. Something changes in my blind, adrenaline-fuelled haze of panic. Fear turns to anger and panic turns to determination. Wrapping my hand around the back of his neck, I pull him close, driving the blade into any available spot. I hate him. I want him dead. A ragged scream slips from my throat as I stab him over and over, finding a certain satisfaction in every single blow. I keep going until my arm aches, and I can no longer breathe properly.

The light blinks on, and all I see is red. Blood. So much blood.

"Lila." Someone says my name on a whispered breath. I shove Nate off me and scramble to my feet. He lies there on my bed, his eyes wide and unseeing, his t-shirt still soaking through with blood like he has sprung a leak. Red stains my bed sheets, my clothes, and my hands.

I wait for the impending tears, the horror, but they are strangely absent. I'm glad he's dead. It's what he deserved. This wasn't wrong. This was justice. I feel the righteousness creeping through me, and for the first time, Judas's words make sense to me. I could almost believe that this is all ordained, part of a higher purpose.

I look at Tiff, Summer, and Trisha who are now all huddled in the doorway.

"I...called the police," Trisha whispers.

"Thank you." My voice is too calm, too controlled.

They're all looking at me like I'm about to either have a breakdown or kill them too.

"Um, Lila, you should put down the knife," Tiff says. I'm still clutching the knife in my hand, blood dripping from the blade, my hands painted red. "Do you want me to call Judas?" She whispers.

I nod mutely, and my knees give way as I collapse to the floor with my back to the bed. I feel empowered, but also numb like my emotions have become so scrambled that I can't find them anymore.

I don't know how long passes... Minutes? Hours?

A man with a tiny torch crouches down in front of me and shines it in my eyes, making me flinch away from him. He moves to touch my neck, but I recoil.

"Delilah, I need you to stand up for me." I blink and look at his face. "That's it, just stand up." I climb to my feet, and he talks to me the entire time as he walks me through the house. I'm hurried outside and into the back of a police car. Of course. I'm a murderer, and murderers get locked up.

Only I don't go to the police station. I'm taken to a hospital where I'm put into a room, stripped and photographed, poked and prodded. I'm finally given a bed, and I sit there with two policemen while they take a statement. They want a blow-by-blow, an exact re-telling of what happened down to the tiniest details. How Nate got in the house. What my previous relationship to him was. On and on it goes, until finally Detective Harford turns up and they leave.

He braces his back to the door, his arms folded over his chest. A deep frown mars his features. "I'm sorry, Miss Thomas." That's it. That's all he says. Then with a shake of his head, he leaves the room.

An hour later and I'm free to go. One of the nurses brings me some jeans and a hoody, courtesy of Tiff. When I step out into the waiting room, Judas is waiting. I spot him immediately as though there's not a single other person in the busy waiting room.

He crosses the room to me and trails his fingers down my cheek. The police only gave me some baby wipes, and I know I still have blood on me. I can feel it crusted onto my skin, clinging to my hairline. His eyes trace over my face, and a soft smile touches his lips. We don't need to say anything. Not here. Taking my hand, he leads me out of the hospital and to his car. We don't speak until we're inside his apartment, standing in the bathroom.

I strip out of the hoody, and then the jeans, dropping them to the bathroom floor. Judas takes in my naked form, his gaze gradually drifting south. I know what I must look like — something out of a nightmare. I also know Judas won't care. He won't judge me. The blood is crusted over my stomach, my chest, my throat, even my legs.

"So perfect." He reaches out, swiping his thumb over the corner of my mouth. "You did it, little lamb. You slayed your demon." Narrowed eyes read my every reaction, looking for weaknesses, but he'll find none. At the hospital, I was just numb, indifferent, but under Judas's watchful gaze, everything becomes so raw again. All that darkness in me rises to the surface for its master, gravitating toward him. In Nate's sacrifice, I can feel my absolution. It's coursing through my veins, swaddling me in the warmth of the virgin's embrace.

"He tried to kill me. He wanted to rape me first." My voice sounds almost robotic. Completely distanced.

Judas closes that tiny gap between us and presses his body to mine. His hands cup my cheeks, and he tilts my head back, forcing me to meet his gaze. "But he didn't."

"No."

He strips out of his shirt, then his trousers, before leading me into the shower. The hot water washes over me and turns crimson before swirling down the drain in a morbid whirlpool.

Those beautiful blue eyes lock with mine as he strokes over my cheek, my jaw; my throat. "So beautiful," he whispers.

Pushing on tiptoes, I press my lips to his. I need him to ground me, to roll in the depravity with me. Maybe I should feel some kind of remorse or horror, but I don't, because as I stand here, covered in blood and staring into his eyes, all I see is adoration.

I kiss him again, but this time he rams me against the tile, his lips coming down hard over mine. There's a sudden air of desperation, a frantic kind of need. His hands are everywhere, claiming, branding, and possessing me in the most reverent of ways. We've always been electric, but this is more. So much more. Everything has changed. I believe. In God, in him, in us. It feels like he's worshipping me, welcoming me into his own personal temple.

"Baptise me," I beg against his lips. He pulls back, meeting my gaze. "Right here. Right now."

"Ah, but that would wash away your sins, and you wear them so beautifully."

"Then don't. Skip that part."

He smiles. "Oh, I'll baptise you, little lamb."

He lifts his hand and draws the cross on my forehead, and the silence of the action is permeated only by the sound of water crashing over tile, our mingled breaths — two hearts beating together.

His lips crash against mine with so much hunger that it steals my breath. Fingers grip my thighs, lifting me and wrenching them apart. And then he's buried inside me. My head falls back against the wall and a moan slips from my lips.

Judas fucks me like he's trying to crawl inside me, as though our souls could be bound anymore than they already are. And I feel it, the inexplicable pull, the absolute knowledge that I'm now every bit as stained as him. I no longer fear the darkness. I embrace it because he's there.

"Delilah Thomas," he nips my earlobe. "I baptise you in the name of the Father." His teeth sink into my neck, and his fingers wrap around my wrists, pinning them above my head as he drives into me. He's reaching into my soul, picking out all the little bits that once made me who I was and pulling on them. "And of the son." Another deep thrust and that telltale tingle of pleasure starts to work through my body. I'm breaking apart, willingly surrendering to him, to his God, to everything that we could be. The pressure builds until I'm teetering on that blissful edge, willing to jump and knowing he'll catch me. "And of the holy spirit," he growls. And I fall, toppling endlessly into nothing but warmth. I'm cleansed, born anew, sculpted into his perfect other half, just as God created Eve for Adam. Everything I was before ceases to exist until I'm simply his.

And here we are, two damned souls bound together, the blood of my last sin still trickling in watery pink lines over my skin. Nothing can tear us apart now. Nothing.

It's only once we're in bed, with the first rays of dawn creeping through the window that we finally speak rationally.

"How did he get out?" I ask, staring at the ceiling.

He grabs my waist and pulls me onto my side to face him. "They convinced him to turn on the Italians. They allowed him a few hours bail before he went into witness protection. He was supposed to be watched..."

"But he wasn't?"

His eyes flash with something depraved. "I paid them off."

Closing my eyes, I roll onto my back. "You wanted him to kill me?" A deep stabbing pain takes up residence behind my ribs.

"No, little lamb. I wanted to create you." He rolls on top of me, his hand cupping my face. "You feel it don't you? The power?" I nod. "He hurt you, Delilah."

"I know."

"And now look at you. You're drowning in sin, like an angel of death." His lips brush over mine. "I simply handed you retribution. I had faith in you." I reach up, scratching my nails over his neck. He's right. "And now everything is perfect. We're perfect."

He kisses me, slow and deep, stirring my emotions back to life before he pulls away.

"Wait here." I frown as I watch him climb from the bed and disappear. A few seconds later he comes back with something clutched in his hand. When he opens his palm, I simply stare at the small knife sitting there.

"Judas?"

"Take the sin, little lamb. Wear it."

"I thought it was to mar your body so as not to mar your soul? What if I want my soul marred?"

"That's Saint. I think of mine as an external representation of my soul. I don't hide what I am. I embrace it." I take the knife from his palm, and he perches on the edge of the bed, watching me intently. "Consider it a wedding present from you to me, little lamb."

"What?"

"I love you, little lamb." I suck in a sharp breath. "You're my perfect other half. Mine in every way, and I will profess it before God himself. Marry me."

And how could I say no? Why would I? I'm his: mind, body, heart and soul. He owns every fibre of me. He made me, created me — moulded me. I trust him with everything that I am.

I place the knife in his hand and grab his wrist, tugging it close to my chest. The point of the knife pricks against my skin.

"Yes. I'll marry you, Judas. Now cut me." And he does, dragging the knife over my skin, carving himself onto my body like a brand that I'll never escape.

EPILOGUE
SAINT

GLANCING AT MY WATCH, I let out a heavy breath and ascend the steps of St Mary's church.

I have no idea why I've been summoned, and I wouldn't be here if the request had come from anyone but Mother. Walking down the aisle, I see Mother, my father and Judas all huddled together in front of the Virgin.

"What is the meaning of this?" I ask.

They all look at me, but it's Mother who rushes forward, pulling me into an embrace that I don't return. Of all my family, she's the only one I have a true fondness for. She is righteous, a devout Catholic, blessed in the eyes of God. My father and brother are sinners, and Judas is the worst of them all, mocking the church, shitting on all that it stands for. Preaching the word of God while sinning under his very roof.

"Judas has an announcement to make." She's smiling like she's just won the lottery, and there's only one thing I can think of that would make her happy like that — the possibility of grandchildren.

"I'm getting married," Judas says, and Mother squeals, flapping her hands around and getting teary.

I hold Judas's gaze, staring him down until I watch him squirm. "And who, pray tell is the unfortunate woman?" Though, of course, I don't need to ask. I turn at the sound of footsteps over the stone floor of the church.

A woman steps through the door, the sunlight spilling around her like a holy apparition. As she moves further inside, I see a cream dress, not white, that stops just above her knees. Dark hair tumbles around her shoulders in soft waves, contrasting with pale skin. She's pretty. Delilah Thomas. Of course, I know exactly who she is. I wouldn't ask my brother to kill her, and then not look into every sordid inch of her pathetic life. She's a nobody. Average in every way. Another blonde girl trails behind her, smiling at everyone and ducking into a pew on the other side of the aisle.

Delilah looks at my brother, and her eyes get that glaze to them. She's like a crack whore just looking for a hit. I smile. Oh, he's good. He's got her tangled up so tightly she thinks he's God himself. Yes, I can see the sins clinging to her like a cloak. She reeks of Judas's blasphemy.

When I look at my brother, his gaze swings to me, a smug smile pulling at his lips. And I wonder. She's his sin, my kill for him to make. But there are rules, exceptions, family being one. So he's going to marry her to save her? How sweet. How pathetic. Not to mention pointless. Why?

She reaches him and takes his hand. Another priest steps out from somewhere, and I take a seat on the pew next to my mother. She hiccups, wiping at tears as they repeat vows to each other. I watch intently; the way Judas looks at her as he professes to love and cherish her. Oh, this is too good. He actually loves her. I wasn't sure my brother was capable — after all, we are so very much alike. He's weak for her.

And so like her namesake, Delilah who cut off Samson's hair and stole his strength, she is his weakness. Interesting.

"Oh." Mother clutches at her chest as they kiss. "I'm so happy for him. She'll make an honest man out of him."

"Do you even know the girl?"

"She seems very sweet, Saint. Now be nice."

I don't know why she wastes her breath, or why she thinks such requests will be heeded. She knows better by now. Standing up, Mother rushes forward as soon as Judas and Delilah pull apart. She pulls the girl into a hug and Father shakes Judas hand. Then my brother is strolling towards me, that smug grin still in place.

"She's supposed to be dead," I say.

"Yes, but now she's family."

I almost respect him for it. Almost. "Well played." I step closer to him, dropping my voice. "But now you owe me two sins."

"You can only have one..."

"I'm changing the rules." He opens his mouth to speak, no doubt to tell me I can't. "And I can. Tread carefully, brother. You have a weak spot now." I nod towards Delilah who is lingering next to my mother still. Judas's jaw tenses, and I smile. "Two sins, brother. Enjoy your honeymoon. I'll be by soon to seal that second debt in blood."

His eyes meet mine, a tentative truce passing between us. He has no idea. He owes me, and I intend to cash in.

*****

How will Saint cash in his sins? Find out what Judas' brother does next in THE SAINT. FREE in KU. Download HERE.

If you like a touch of psychopathic madness, you'll love ABSOLUTION; the story of a religiously fanatic serial killer and the man she becomes obsessed with. Absolution is now FREE in KU for a limited time. Download HERE.

"It's Fifty Shades on crack with an eight ball injected straight into your brain whilst having electric shock therapy." - **Malebox (Totally Booked Blog) Five stars.**

SAINT EXCERPT

The heavy scent of wood polish, incense and dust wraps around me, bringing me a rare sense of peace and familiarity. "Forgive me father for I have sinned."

There's a heavy sigh from the other side of the lattice divider followed by a pause. "Son, you've been here every day for the last four days. There is only so much forgiveness you can be given. It's not accumulative."

But I need it to be. I need some divine intervention. "I didn't tell you my sin."

. . .

"God, the Father of mercies, through the death and resurrection of his Son has reconciled the world—"

"I killed a man." Silence. "I killed him because he hurt her."

I count eight heavy heartbeats thrumming against my ribs before he answers. "And do you repent?" Father Maxwell asks, his voice barely above a whisper. He sees me, I know it. For the first time, he truly see's the monster that I keep leashed. I'm no longer just the strange boy who has come to his church for the last thirty years, or even the mysterious and unsettling man he's come to know. That niggling feeling of danger he gets when he's near me, the one he's always told himself is so irrational finally all makes sense. I'm a killer, a sinner, a predator living amongst his prey. I can almost hear it all clicking into place in his mind.

"No," I answer truthfully. "I'm not sorry that I killed him." I feel nothing, only the troubling disappointment that God will judge me and finally see the truth. That I am so very wrong, that without his guidance, I would have unleashed all my dark urges on his children a long time ago. I walk the fine line between despising people and fearing that I will go to hell for my very nature. *Bad boys go to hell*, my mothers voice whispers in my ear.

I hear the priest take a shaky breath. "Then you cannot be truly absolved of sin."

·   ·   ·

"I'm destined for the fires of hell," I murmur.

He takes a shaky breath, the sound like a gun shot in the silence of the confessional. "Unless you truly repent in your soul."

Pushing to my feet, I grab the curtain, pausing for a moment. "I have no soul."

And without a soul, what do heaven or hell really matter?

———

ABOUT THE AUTHOR

Sign up to my newsletter and stay up to date with new releases:
Join the Mailing List

Dark Mafia Series:
    Kiss of Death series
    Collateral Series
    Touch of Death Series
    Wrong Series
    Bad Series

Standalones

Super Dark and Fucked Up:
    Absolution
    The Pope
    The Game

Gritty High School Romance:
    No Prince
    No Good

Taboo Erotic Romance:
    Dirty Boss

Website: www.lplovell.co.uk

Facebook: https://www.facebook.com/lplovellauthor

Instagram: @lp_lovell

TikTok: @authorlplovell

Goodreads: https://www.goodreads.com/author/show/7850247.LP_Lovell

Amazon: https://www.amazon.com/LP-Lovell/e/B00NDZ61PM

Printed in Great Britain
by Amazon

48122344R00142